Juwell & Precious

Platinum Teen Series

Introduces…

THE AB-SOLUTE TRUTH

By

Juwell   &   Precious

This novella is a work of fiction. Any resemblance to real people, living or dead, actual events, establishments, is intended to give the fiction a sense of reality and authenticity. Other names, characters, places, and incidents are either products of the author's imagination or are used fictitiously.

Precioustymes Entertainment

229 Governors Place, #138
Bear, DE 19701
(302) 594-9949
Email: precioustymesent@aol.com
Website: www.precioustymes.com

Library of Congress Control Number: 2005903702
ISBN# 0-9729325-4-2
Cover Design: www.ccwebdev.com
Content Editor: Jahmya Ross

First Trade Paperback Edition Printing January 2006 - Printed in U.S.

Platinum Teen Series

Dedications

Juwell

Mom Dukes, Sue, Davana, Caleb, Ke'maine, Britney, Devon, Craig, Eric, Derrick, Jr., Lee, Janice, Christina, Chanel, KeYonna, Angel, Debbra, Ricky, Precola, Ebony, Shannon, LaToya, Grandma, Grandpa, Harold (RIP), Runk (RIP), Sibo (RIP), Judy, Jerry, Darryl, Jill, Mike, Vivian, Scooter, Rick, Rob, James and my hundreds of lil' cousins.

Precious

Jahmya, Mecca, Mehki, Lamotte, Jasmine, Keontai, Mikeira, Ki-Ki, Sabrina, Alexis, Starr, Jade, Rhythm, Robynn, Jayvonna, Brittany, Gloria, Marshay, Porsha, Yakira, Chelsie, Sateyai, Mira, Santanna, Teniesha, Honey, Charnay, Jazz, Nadirah, Capathia, Isaiah, Jaiquone, Josiah, Kenyatta, DeArtis, Jamir, Darnell, Brandon, Ali, Wuesi, Hashim, Kenny, Laron, Shawnay, Kierra, Justine and Dejah.

Intro

What's up y'all? They call me Abdul, but my real name; my birth given name is Christopher Parker. I'm a young Scrappy, only 17 years old, but I'm a senior in high school and straight like that... I'm the man. I'm on the school's basketball team; to me, I am the team. Feel me? I'm a pretty boy, plus I'm the best-dressed brotha in the building. The girls all love me to death, and the guys either want to be me, or want to be around me. I'm that dude!

I live with my mother, Sara Parker, my father, Manuel Parker Sr., and my lil' brother, Manuel Parker, Jr., who we call Manny. He's a year younger than me. We had an older brother named Tyrone Parker who used to be a Probation Officer. He was killed on a home visit by an ex-con who violated his probation. The man didn't want to go back to jail and refused to cooperate. The scene got ugly when he pulled out his gun and fired a shot directly into my brother's heart, killing him with one bullet. Two lives were lost that day, my brother's and the ex-con who was killed by my brother's partner, Mark Stone. Tyrone was a Muslim, which is how I became Muslim and was renamed, Abdul. Although, our family is a Christian family, Tyrone and I were the only Muslim members in the family. We lost Tyrone at the age of 22, only two years ago. It was a painful blow to our family, but our love for each other helped us to deal with our loss.

Mark started coming around to check on us after my brother died; we started calling him Uncle Mark after that. He knew how much love Tyrone had for us and wanted to help any way he could. He was around us so much that he felt like a blood relative.

My mother and father own a small Mom & Pop Grocery store and we live on the two floors above it. They owned the store years before we were born. It was in our family for two decades. Everybody that knows us or knows about us thinks our family is rich. Most people in the hood have the misconception that if you own a store, regardless of how small, meager or the time frame of the existence of the store may be; you must either be rich or well off. When in fact, our status is far from that. I mean we make ends meet. Meaning, we don't rely on public assistance for income. This too, of course, keeps the state out of our personal and family business. It's nothing like having nosey Social Workers in your business. Understand though, we struggle like everybody else in our hood. I even sell a little weed in my spare time, which is how I can afford to be the best dressed in school. I know it's wrong, but sometimes you gotta do what you gotta do. If I were to get caught, it would probably scare me straight – I can't lie! It's also how I bought myself my white beauty – a white Ford Tempo. Now don't get me wrong, I don't have to sell weed. I do it because I choose to. Not one of my smarter decisions, I admit, but I don't plan on making a career out of it. I'm going to college to play ball, then to the NBA. Yeah, I plan to be Allen Iverson, Lebron James and like the legendary Michael Jordan of the NBA. Yes, Christopher (Abdul) Parker, #12, starting point guard, M.V.P., that's me!

Chapter One

The hands on the clock must need some oil or something, 'cause they are ticking slowly as if I don't have somewhere to be, I thought to myself while sitting in the back of the classroom, observing nothing but the clock. This was the last period for the day after which, I'd be headed to basketball practice. I don't make it a habit of not paying attention in class. The nerd in me wouldn't allow that; but being that I was three quarters of the way through my senior year, who cared if I fell back and chilled in Chemistry class. Especially, since I've maintained a high grade point average all year. I was definitely graduating.

My mind was drifting back and forth from basketball practice to Porsha, but it wasn't practice that was occupying my thoughts of getting out of class, Porsha was; my new young girl, a freshman at that. Man, I know what you're saying, but she's stacked like four fluffy pancakes. Some grown women couldn't even touch her curves. Besides her physical features, she was the cutest girl in school. This made plenty of girls hate. It was unheard of for a senior to make a freshman his main girl, but Porsha was an exception. We've been dating the majority of the school year and still we haven't had sex yet. You heard me right, I didn't hit yet. Most of the students thought we were getting it on, even her girls; but we weren't. I put on a real front in front of everyone like we were though. My lil' brother Manny is getting more on his end, than I am on mine. It was Porsha and I that hooked them up. At 16, Manny was two years older than Kera. She's a cutie also, but she wasn't on Porsha's level. She was sneaky and fast with pulling her pants down. Manny didn't play on the team, but he traveled with us like he did. He stayed straight pimpin' in the bleachers, trying to recruit some new chicks.

The truth of the matter was I liked the chase that Porsha took me on. It's what drew me to her the most. I could have sex with any girl in the school mainly, (I never said I was a virgin) but Porsha was a challenge. Porsha always showed up for basketball practice, as did many other girls trying to get at me. Today, I was trying to get at her to sneak in a few kisses before practice started.

Looking up from my pile of schoolwork I noticed a note being passed back by a student, headed toward me. It was from my boy Nat, who was sitting in the front row. He was asking me what I was going to do after class. I drew a basketball on the paper and sent it back, figuring he'd get the picture. You get it – get the picture?

When the bell rang signaling the end of the period, I couldn't get out of the classroom fast enough. Nat was waiting for me in the hallway.

"Man, I couldn't wait to get up out of there," I said to him.

"I feel you. I'm thinking about going with you to practice," he replied.

"What's there to think about?" I asked, walking down the hall on my way to the gym.

"I want to know if the cheerleaders are gonna be there. You know how I do," he smiled.

I laughed saying, "Yeah, they're gonna be down there and yeah, I do know you."

"What's that supposed to mean?"

"Nothing," I answered, not wanting to hurt his feelings. Nat was one of those guys that girls just didn't flock to. I didn't know why, I just knew it to be true. Yet, he refused to aim low. He always went after the best looking girls in the school, including the cheerleaders that kept passing him always saying, "One day they'll all be chasing after me. Watch!"

We made our way to the gym where I changed in the locker room into my practice gear. When I came out, all the ballers were ready to get practice going. The coach split us up into two teams – shirts against the skins. The girls in the stands were excited by the display of flesh and muscle. Manny made his way over to me before the game began. He was a fill-in for the shirts side. I was on the skins team.

"What up Ab?" Manny asked, "Have you checked the stands?"

"Nah, not really. What am I supposed to be checking for? I was hoping to see my shorty before practice started, but I didn't." My eyes scanned the stands, which were seated with mostly females.

"Third row from the top, on your left," Manny said, while playing it smoothly. After he pointed that out, I spotted whom he was talking about. It was Porsha and Kera. Kera must have skipped out of school because she went to our rivalry high school, Newark High. They got out of school the same time we did and it took like thirty minutes to get to Howard Vo-tech from Newark, by car. They were both looking real good, but in my eyes, Porsha was really representing. I winked in her direction and in return, she blew me a kiss.

The game got underway with my archrival, Jamal Waters, playing point for the shirts. I used to be the number

9

one starting point guard until Jamal enrolled at our school. He was claiming hood status, but was a prep school dude living in the 'burbs before he came to Howard Vo-tech. Coach had pulled me back as a secondary point guard. It crushed me at first, but I was willing to fight for my starting spot again. This switch did create some hate in my blood for this dude who spoke like he was the man on my team.

Jamal and I went head to head shooting jumpers in each other's faces. I killed him when I did my famous A.I. crossover move that landed me two points down low. He was pissed at me for showing off like that and the other players watched as the tension built between the two of us. The game had become Abdul versus Jamal, not shirts versus skins. Jamal got the ball under the post and I played defense to the best of my ability like scouts were out recruiting. This dude was not about to jerk me in front of my girl. Jamal bounced the ball back high off the dribble and tried to fake to the left and slid down on his leg from the sweat that was dripping on the court. Right in the middle of the game, he pulled a hamstring. An injury like this was serious. We knew he wouldn't be able to play point when we played Newark in a few days. With Jamal out the game and Kyle taking his place with the shirts, we (the skins) destroyed them. After the game the coach gathered us together to give us that victory speech. Which wasn't out of the ordinary, except Principal Banks was with him.

"Good game today Christopher." The coach gave me my props. "You really impressed me tonight."

"Thanks coach," I gleamed.

"Don't thank me yet. Thank me after we beat Newark High."

"What do you mean?" I asked, assuming what was coming after that.

"I mean you're starting next game."

"Coach, how can you do that?   He's..." Jamal protested.

"Don't start it Jamal, you're hurt – out with an injury son. There's not much you can do with a pulled hamstring."

"I'll be straight before the big game." Jamal hoped to get another chance at it.

"Not true son, as it stands, Christopher will start in your place next game. Now, this discussion is closed," Coach firmly declared.

Jamal shot a look in my direction that would've killed an innocent bystander, if I'd ducked.   I played the back, knowing it was eating him up.

"Well, on a lighter note, I have some good news for the seniors in the group, " Principal Banks cut in.   "There are going to be a few college scouts looking for recruits next game.   That's right, scholarships will be on the table, so I suggest you guys play like you want one. And, not like Jamal today, showing out, risking his career because of a macho ego."

"Coach please, this might be my only chance at a full ride. You can't bench me with scouts in the stands!" All that smack Jamal talk, he was crying like a girl.

"You should have thought about that," Coach parted from his lips.

After the announcement, coach dismissed us. The rest of the team made their way to the showers, but I stepped to Manny for the car keys then, headed in the stands to chat with my girl.

"What's up ma?" I greeted her.   She was looking good in her tight Lady Enyce jeans and shirt to match.

"Good game, boo. You was doing your thing out there," she said, encouragingly.

"Only 'cause you were watching, shorty," I said grabbing her by the waistline.

"We need a ride home, Abdul."

"We who?" I played around with her.

"Kera and I."

Then Kera cut in rudely, "I'm saying Ab, why your brother gon' just walk to the locker room like he didn't see me waiting out here for him?"

"You'll have to ask him that Kera. And, how are you doing?" I asked sarcastically while handing my car keys to Porsha.

"I'm alright. Sorry, Abdul. I'm just saying."

"What are these for?" Porsha asked, holding up the keys to the car.

"They're called keys to use for a car," I dumbed her down.

"I mean, why are you giving them to me, Mr. Smarty?" Smacking my arm playfully, she giggled.

"So you and Kera can wait in the car for us."

"You must think I'm stupid Abdul. Are you trying to get rid of me? You think I don't see all these girls up in here lounging around?" Porsha's jealous streak started to kick in. Although, I sometimes enjoyed her jealous fits, I wasn't in the frame of mind for that at this time.

"Do what you want Porsha. I'll be out in a minute, alright?" I left her there, making my way to the showers with the rest of my teammates.

After I showered, I changed into my new beige camouflage State Property outfit.

"Are they still out there?" Manny asked referring to Porsha and Kera while hovering over me with his gym bag slung over his shoulder.

Looking at Manny, I saw my dad in him. They had the same small chinky eyes, narrow chin and dark completed skin. Everyone said that Manny is like my twin, but I don't see it. He's more like my dad's twin.

"I don't know," I answered him. "I told them to wait in the car."

"Good move, bro! I can't get no airplay with the cheerleaders when Kera is constantly hanging on my neck like a platinum chain," he whined.

"Oh yo', I heard you were in stolen car last night." I watched to see if his eyes twitched which would have meant he was lying. A few friends from the projects had put me on to this. "Don't make me have to beat you down like I used to when we were younger, duke." It was hard to keep Manny away from criminal activity, when he knew that I was selling weed. I even bought him clothes whenever I purchased them for myself. I felt guilty that my little brother was following behind my lead.

"Calm down. I needed a whip (car) to take Kera out last night. It's not like you was gonna let me drive yours."

"You're right," I agreed, then added, "But one night of joy riding isn't worth a few years in jail young'n'."

"Ai'ight Ab," Manny said walking away.

"Don't ai'ight me! Just don't do it again."

On the way out the locker room, we both cut through the gym to see if Porsha and Kera were still out there. I noticed that they accepted my offer and waited out in the car. I stopped to talk with Nat and Manny stopped to talk to some

13

girl named Morgan who he'd been dealing with for a few weeks.

"So Ab," Nat inquired. "How do you feel about college? Have you ever thought about going?"

"Who hasn't? I just never thought I'd be able to afford it."

"You never thought about a scholarship?"

"Not really, I'm a secondary point guard. What scout would notice me sitting on the bench? When I started that was another story. I had in my mind that scholarships would be coming from every well known Division I college."

"I bet they'll be coming now that you're starting again. Watch! It's primetime baby!"

"I'm going to make sure that they do, even if they don't want to," I said laughing. "Yo man, I'm up outta here. I got to drop these chicks off." I told him while waving my hand to Manny, signaling him to come on. He gave the girl Morgan a long affectionate hug (feeling on all her curves) and ran to catch up with me as I walked outside of the gym.

When we approached my car, Porsha climbed out of the driver's seat into the passenger's. I got behind the wheel and Manny hopped in the back with Kera. Before anyone could start running their mouths I turned the radio on full blast, allowing the four 12" subwoofers that I had in the trunk of the car to drown everybody out.

My mind was running with thoughts of the scouts and the strong possibilities of a college scholarship. It was almost too much to digest. Destiny had thrown me a weird twist of fate. If I played my game right, and I was, one signature could get me a full ride.

14

From the corner of my eye I saw Porsha reaching for the radio. I know she couldn't take riding home without conversation.

"Abdul, what are you and Manny doing after school the day after tomorrow?"

"I don't know, why?"

"Because, my house will be empty," she hinted, smiling at me.

"Word? Where's your moms gonna be, on another outing? She's never home from what you tell me."

"You should be happy about that. Are you coming over or what?"

"I'll think about it and let you know." I didn't want to pressure her into doing anything that she didn't want to, but if she pressed the issue, I would be there.

"Your loss!" I detected a lot of meaning in her last comment. Her devilish grin said I was accurate. I believe she was hinting that we should fool around – alone!

"Well I'll be there," I confirmed. She was the one who pressed the issue... I didn't.

I checked the rearview mirror and caught a glimpse of both Manny and Kera hugged up in the back.

Chapter Two

The following day during lunchtime, I went out to eat with a few of my team members. It was kind of a pre-game celebration for our game against Newark in a few days. Manny, Kyle, Robbie, Jason and even Nat were all in attendance at the greasy burger joint near our school.

"To Howard High, the Detroit Pistons of high school ball," Robbie announced while holding up his paper cup of Root beer for a toast.

"To Howard High," we all chimed and tapped soft drink cups with Robbie.

"Yo, I met the baddest chick on this coast, and she's really feelin' the kid," Kyle stated to everyone.

"Where'd you meet her?" Manny asked doubtfully.

"At the library."

"Yeah, that's how you get your hunt on Kyle," Nat added.

"What's this cat talking about?" Manny asked jokingly.

"I'm talking about church, the library, even the doctor's office. Those are the best places to meet bad girls," he analyzed.

"Yeah, you're right. If you're meeting girls in the doctor's office, you need some church and the clinic in your life," I added causing everyone to burst out into laughter.

"What's her name, Kyle?" Jason asked.

"Dymond, Dymond in the Rough," Kyle answered, catching my absolute attention. That name rang a bell for me.

"Does she go to Newark High?" I asked him.

"How did you know that?" Kyle asked, "Don't tell me she's on your long list of accomplishments."

"No, no, but her cousin is. Dymond is Porsha and Kera's cousin." I relieved him of his worry.

"For real? What does she look like Ab?" Manny asked, interested to see if Kyle was exaggerating or not.

"She's a dime, but she's on point. Stuck up, though." I had to keep it real with him.

"She talked to me, even flirted with me," Kyle said in her defense. "She can't be that stuck up."

"Yeah, and that's about all she's gonna do with you," I assured him.

"I'm saying Kyle, you can find out tomorrow," Manny said.

"How?"

"We're going to Porsha's house after school tomorrow to hang out. Her moms won't be there, feel me?" Manny offered a chance for him to find out on his own.

"I don't know if I can get Dymond over there. I just met her," he confessed.

"Man, stop punkin' out. We'll have Kera and Porsha take care of that. You just handle your business when we get there and stay out of my way," I said to him.

Porsha had me on standby for so long, but it was finally going to pay off. I didn't want nothing or nobody to interfere with that.

"I got you Ab, just get Dymond there," Manny said.

"So Abdul," Jason butted in. "You got lucky yesterday. It's not often when you lose a starting spot to get it back. Especially when the fill in is better than you."

I brushed that off. "Yeah, my worst enemy gets hurt at the most perfect time to help my future. Now, that's fate for real."

"Whatever it was, your boy Jamal was heated," Kyle added.

"Heated ain't the word, especially when he heard about the scouts that are coming next game." Manny reminded us.

"Oh, you know I was loving the look on his face," I said glad that it pissed him off.

"So what college would you like to attend?" Robbie asked.

"Harvard," I joked to get a laugh.

"Yeah right! Now let's talk realistically," Jason stated with disbelief.

"How about Duke? They have a strong team," Manny suggested.

"He needs to get on a weak team so he can shine," Kyle attempted to analyze my career.

"But weak teams don't get national attention or media coverage," Manny argued. "What would be the point then? He could shine all he wanted but without national exposure most ball players get overlooked."

18

This began a debate between us about what team was good for me and why. I let them go back and fourth about ten minutes before I cut in.

"Excuse me, any of you ever heard about the word curriculum?" They all sat silently on deaf ears staring at me for the answer.

"Of course, but what's that have to do with what we're talking about?" Robbie inquired.

"Doe-doe brain, I'm playing basketball to get a scholarship for college; not going to college solely for basketball. In case you haven't noticed, I've always been focused on my education. If I get to the NBA, that's what's up, but what happens if I get injured like Jamal did? I'll still have my education to fall back on." They were all young boys with the exception of Nat and maybe Robbie, who were my age. So, future plans weren't on the top of their list yet.

"Why do this guy always turn a fun conversation into something serious?" I guess Jason thought I was all work and no play. This gave me the opportunity to mess with them.

"Because I'm the elder in the group. The voice of reason for you young folks," I conveyed with my mature intellectual facial expression, trying my hardest not to laugh.

"Elder?" my brother questioned. "Man, we ain't a tribe in some village in the jungles of Africa."

"Yeah, but if you enjoy the benefits of hanging around me, you'll have to take pleasure in all the positive messages that I have to offer. What I look like hanging with y'all young boys and not feeding your brains with positive input?"

"Get real," Manny said with trouble written all over his face.

"Yo', I gotta roll. I'll catch up with y'all later. My class starts in 15 minutes," Kyle said while gathering his things and tossing his trash in the nearest wastebasket.

"Yeah, me too. I gotta get my brains fed with positive input," Manny said mimicking what I said causing everyone to laugh on our way out of the burger joint.

"Whether you find yourselves in a Wall Street boardroom hoping to make millions or behind the wall in a parole board hoping to get out of jail, you'll remember all the positive advice I gave you lil bro'." I promised him that and Nat nodded his head in agreement.

Chapter Three

We walked back to school together, but our group dispersed as we entered the crowd of students going inside the school. Manny and I remained together after spotting our uncle. Uncle Mark was brown-skin; about 6 feet even and very muscular; which I guess came in handy in his line of work. He was also one of those really hairy men. He had hair on his hands, his back, his ears and protruding out his nose. It was fitting though, because regardless of how menacing he seemed, he was a big teddy bear. And, the only Uncle we had. Even though he wasn't our real kin-folk (family).

"Hey nephews!"

"What's up Unc? Who are you here to pick up?" Manny pried.

"None of these young girls want an old furry man," I joked with him.

"Oh, it's comedian day rugrats?" Mark retaliated.

"Naa, what's on your mind?" I asked seriously after realizing that uncle Mark never came up to our school unless someone was in trouble. "I need to have a word with you Abdul," he stated.

"About what?" Manny asked.

"Is your name Abdul?"

"No."

"Then, take your butt in school Manuel," He shoved Manny towards the classrooms.

"Come on Uncle Mark, I told you about calling out my whole name in public! That's ain't cool."

"What have you been teaching that boy?" Mark asked me.

"The same stuff you teach me," I replied.

"I doubt that. You still have a lot to learn."

"That's not what you came out here to talk about," I told him.

"You're right, first I want you to know I just spoke with Coach Holland; he told me about the scouts. Are you ready for that?"

"You can come back after school and play one on one with me to find out if I'm ready."

"That's not what I meant, besides we both know you're not ready for me on the court."

"Bet something!" Then, I paused puzzled, "What you did you mean anyway?"

"I meant college, are you ready for college?" he clarified. I took a minute to reflect on what he'd asked me; coming from Unc, I knew this was one of those trick questions.

"Why wouldn't I be ready for college? School is school," I shoot back at him. "It's all the same."

"I hope you don't really believe that, Abdul. There's a big difference between college and high school."

22

"Yeah, I know that," I answered, tired of the subject.

"I hope so,' 'cause you won't only be going to college for yourself, your little brother will be watching. He idolizes everything you do and you have to set an example for him."

"Don't I always? He's on the team because I am… he goes to school faithfully 'cause I do. He…"

"He sells drugs 'cause you do," Uncle Mark blurted out unexpectedly, catching me off guard. *How did he find that out?* I thought to myself. And I wondered did he know for sure or was he taking shots in the dark? If he did know, how was he gonna handle this? I mean he's my uncle and all that, but he's still law enforcement even if he ain't a cop.   He's still affiliated with them.

"He doesn't sell drugs."

"Maybe not, at least not yet," he said, "but you do."

That wasn't a question and he didn't answer unsure. There it was; he put it out there. The real reason he came down to my school was out the bag and what a head banger it was.

"Where'd you hear that?" I stalled, playing stupid.

"Does it matter? It's true!" He made a direct statement not a question.

He took my silence to mean that I wasn't going to answer him and he was right. I wasn't gonna deny or confirm nothing. The phrase *'you have a right to remain silent'* kept playing over and over in my head.

Uncle Mark must've read my mind 'cause he said, "Come on, Abdul. I'm not stupid and I'm not asking you. I'm telling you that I know you've been selling drugs; weed to be exact."

"What? How?" I stammered trying to think of an exit, any way out of this.

23

"The only work you do is at your parent's store and I know they ain't giving you enough money to afford the clothes and jewelry you've been buying."

Trapped like a rat, I asked, "Do my parents know?"

"Not yet. How long do you think you could get away with this before I found out?" he asked calmly.

"I wasn't planning on doing it long. I'm just making a little change, not trying to get rich. No harm, nothing foul." I defended my actions.

"It's called 'crime' and you might as well be trying to get rich, 'cause when you get caught your entire life could go out the window... head first."

"I won't get caught," I was sure I wouldn't. My game was tight.

"Why? Cause you're so smart and I guess, so careful? If I found out, what makes you think the police won't find out?"

"You're gonna call the cops on me?" I asked worried.

"Of course not, why would I do that? Especially since you're not going to do it anymore. There's nothing to tell, right?" I couldn't tell if he was giving me an ultimatum or not, but I did get the point.

"Nope, there's nothing to tell." I lied, knowing that I was gonna keep hustling; I just had to be more on the down low. *I respect Uncle Mark, but he doesn't understand the life of a teenager in the hood,* I thought to myself, still decided to continue to do me.

"Listen, Abdul... I love you like family and I won't tell you anything wrong. And like I said before, Manny is watching; it's only a matter of time before he follows your lead. He's your little brother and he's your responsibility; just like you were Tyrone's responsibility." My mind flooded with

24

thoughts and images of my late brother. He continued on, "Opportunity has presented itself. Doors are opening for you; it's too late in the game to start messing up your future for something so stupid!"

"I feel you Unc; you're right. I gotta get to class. I'll call you after school if you want me to," I offered, trying to get up out of there. Uncle Mark had a way of seeing through dishonesty and I was being nothing but dishonest with a mixture of sincerity.

"No need, I made my point. I'll drop by to see y'all at your big game. Oh, just so you know, a drug dealer's retirement place is in a jail cell." He gave me a hug and made himself very clear about the consequences of being a drug dealer.

"I love you, Unc."

"I love you too, Abdul. Keep in mind what we talked about." As he walked off, I felt as though I had just dodged a bullet, not knowing that I'd be running into a few if I didn't get my act together.

Chapter Four

.   **The next day,** I cut school early to hit the mall for a few outfits. I took Porsha with me for company, but she managed to walk out the mall with a few bags of her own; my treat of course. I opened the car doors and began loading the bags into the backseat, as Porsha stood idly by making small talk.

The plan was to pick up Manny, Kyle, Kera and Dymond from Newark High; that's if Kera could talk Dymond into coming along. After which we would all head over to Porsha's house. I was just wondering to myself – how was I going to fit four people in the back with all those bags? Well, they'd just have to make do, 'cause the bags wouldn't fit in my trunk.

On our ride to Newark High, I felt Porsha watching me and I knew she was going for the radio soon. Just as I suspected, she turned down the radio and stared at me as if she was studying me.

"What Porsha?" I asked, keeping my eyes on the road. I hated when she turned down my music to run her big mouth.

"What's wrong, Ab?"

"How do you figure something's wrong?"

"I'm saying, boo… you've been quiet all day." With a perplexed look on her face, she asked, "Have I done something wrong?"

"Besides messing with my mind – naa; you ain't do nothing wrong. I have more important stuff on my mind."

"Care to share?" she asked persistently trying to get me to talk. Knowing Porsha, I knew she wouldn't stop until we discussed what was bothering me and until we did, she'd be what was bothering me. So I gave in.

"Do you remember my Uncle Mark?"

"Yea; the big hairy guy."

"Whatever. Anyway, he found out that I sell weed and he's connected with the law."

"He's a cop?" she asked.

"No, he's a probation officer; same thing – not really, but really. The point is he stepped to me yesterday and told me to stop selling drugs."

"Wow! Do your parents know?"

"Naa, he said he wouldn't tell them, if I stop."

"So, are you gonna stop?"

"No," I said and she got real quiet. We rode along in silence for about ten minutes, which amazed me. I didn't know she could go so long without talking. Then she broke the silence, "Abdul, do you want to know what I think?" She asked as if I had a choice in the matter; like if I said no, she wouldn't tell me anyway.

"What?" I finally said, inviting the inevitable.

"I think you should stop."

Slightly curious, I asked, "Why is that?"

"Because you really don't need to sell drugs for money. You have parents that care! And, you really don't need the trouble. If everything goes well the next game, you

27

could be off to college soon." She sounded older than her fourteen years.

"That's why you're my shorty; you're an old head in a beautiful young girl's body," I complimented her, reaching for the radio.

"Does that mean you're going to stop?"

"Probably not, and if you touch my radio again – you'll be walking – trust me," I promised and blasted the volume before she could retort any sassy comebacks. Surprisingly, she believed my threats and we rode the rest of the way listening to the new Cassidy CD I had purchased from the mall.

I'ma hustla, I'ma, I'ma hustla homie! Cassidy blazed the track.

When we pulled in front of the school, Manny, Kera, Kyle and Dymond were waiting on us. Everybody greeted one another, then the four of them packed into the back seat of my car. Kyle and Manny had the girls sitting on their laps 'cause my bags didn't leave much room for anything else. *They can thank me later*, I thought to myself, as I switched CD's.

They were all talking amongst each other; I pretty much stayed out of the conversation. Then my song came on, which was perfect for the subject that I discussed with Porsha before the rest of them got in my car. It was the Ja Rule and R. Kelly song that goes, *"If it wasn't for the money, cars, movie stars, jewels and all the things I got, I wonder... would you still want me?"* I sang along loudly. Porsha knew I was singing to her, as did everyone else in the car.

Porsha jumped in my song saying she would still want me. *Of course, she'd say that,* I thought to myself. Before we arrived at Porsha's house, I stopped at McDonalds, knowing she never had anything to eat at her house. I was going to treat

28

everybody, but only Kyle declined my offer. He had some first date fronting to do, so he paid for himself and Dymond.

After McDonald's, we rode to Porsha's house. Porsha invited everyone in as if the whole day wasn't already planned. Only the girl, Dymond was hesitant. It took a minute for them to talk her into the house. Once in the house, I made myself at home. I flopped down on her couch and turned on her big screen T.V. My brother snatched up Kera, leading her off into the backroom; he glanced briefly to wink his eye at me. *Show off!*

Porsha began massaging my shoulders, relaxing me and turning me on at the same time. I looked up into her eyes and signaled to her to get rid of Dymond and Kyle, who were sitting up in our faces looking nervous.

"Dymond, you and Kyle can go upstairs in my room if you want to. My mom won't be home 'til 8:00 tonight and her man won't be back 'til tomorrow morning," Porsha told her uptight cousin.

While Porsha was trying to convince her, I joined on to speed up the process. I pulled Porsha over the couch, onto my lap and asked both Kyle and Dymond for a little privacy. Eventually, they went up to Porsha's bedroom and when they did, it was on. Porsha and I went at it like we never did before.

She let me get to 1st base, 2nd base and I stole 3rd base, being sneaky. And just about when I was about to slide into home plate, she stopped me.

"What's wrong, Porsha?" I whispered as I continued kissing on her neck.

"Hold up, Abdul; wait a minute," she said as she pushed me off her.

"What happened?" I asked baffled and frustrated.

"First of all, you don't even have a condom. You must be crazy boy!" she said loudly.

"I do have a condom. I have a bunch of condoms in my pocket," I pleaded.

"You don't have a condom on. Also, I ain't doing nothing on this couch, they might come out and catch us," she said, pulling her skirt back down over her thighs.

"One question... if you knew you wanted to wait for a bedroom, why did you let them use the only two rooms?"

"They won't be long, Ab. You waited all this time, a few minutes won't kill you." Her tone told me that her mind was made up. I sat back on the couch, pretending to be watching T.V.

"Ab?"

"WHAT?"

"That doesn't mean we can't mess around until we get to my bedroom," she said sweetly. My anger faded and my teenage hormones began raging again. We started back up, but this time before we could get too far, Kyle and Dymond returned back downstairs. The two of them walked past us and out the door. I wasn't too concerned about where they were headed. My mind was on the empty room they just left behind. I pulled my tongue out of Porsha's mouth to say, "Come on."

"Come on, where?" she asked.

"Upstairs to your room," I replied eagerly.

"Abdul, I told you; you can wait until they come out. They won't be up there all night."

"They're not up there anymore; they walked by us a few seconds ago," I said trying to pull her up off of the couch.

"Did they? Where'd they go?" she asked.

"Outside. Are you trying to stall, Porsha?"

"No, I just didn't see them come by."

"That's 'cause you were caught up in the Ab," I said and she laughed as we made our way up the creaky stairs.

Once we hit the door, it was on like popcorn! She let me get my homerun. My parents always told me that intimacy is better when you love the person you're with, but I wasn't sure if I was in love with her like that. The only problem we had was near the end... my condom broke. I was so into it that I didn't stop.

Porsha began panicking when I told her afterwards, "What do you mean it broke?"

"You know what I mean and stop shouting," I said trying to calm her down.

"How could you let that happen?"

"I didn't make the rubber, I bought it," I explained.

"Did you put it on correctly?"

"What kind of question is that? Did you put your socks correctly this morning?" I replied, getting smart right back to her.

She was snapping so much; I didn't even have the time or opportunity to stress the issue.

"Abdul, this isn't funny. I could get pregnant," she said, bringing me back to reality.

"You're not pregnant, stop overreacting," I told her seriously, not finding the situation funny anymore. I was nowhere near being ready to be a father.

"You don't know that... you're not a doctor!"

"Look Porsha, it was an accident; nobody's to blame. We just shared a beautiful moment together, so why mess it up by arguing?" I reasoned with her.

She calmed down. "You're right, Ab. I'm sorry."

"Don't worry about it." I held her for a while, thinking to myself, *I hope she's not pregnant. I don't need that kind of drama right now.*

After some time, we got dressed and drove Kera, Kyle and Dymond home. The following day was the big and I needed all the rest I could get if I was going to impress those scouts. I had already hurled over one obstacle... having sex with Porsha. My next challenge – the big game!

Chapter Five

Today's the day - 'full court Friday' – the big game! I woke up early that morning, before my parents and Manny. I showered, put on my workout gear and my I Pod, and then I went out jogging like Rocky Balboa did in his first *Rocky* movie. Except, in my life, I didn't have the whole city jogging with me and cheering me on. It was just me and my I Pod banging everything from The Game to Mike Jones; which was all the motivation I needed on my trek through the neighborhood and back.

When I returned from my morning jog, my family was up and about. My mother was cooking breakfast, flooding the kitchen with various aromas: eggs, grits, pancakes and sizzle lean.

"Morning, baby. How was your jog?" my mother asked, while handing me a glass of cold orange juice, home-style with bits of pulp in it. I gulped the glass down and replied, "Morning, mom. It was very therapeutic."

"Big words, early in the morning? You must be in high spirits. Are you eating breakfast with us?"

Yea, it's going to be a long strenuous day and I'm going to need all the nourishment I can get."

"That girl, Porsha, called for you. I told her that her little fast behind need to be getting ready for school; not on the phone."

"What did she want?"

"I don't know, your brother spoke to her."

"Where is he?"

"He's in the shower, where I hope you're headed," she said holding her nose jokingly.

On my way upstairs, I passed through the living room where my father was on the couch with his feet on the coffee table reading the newspaper.

"Morning, Dad," I said on my way upstairs.

Looking at his paper, he said, "Hey boy! You make sure you give 'em all you got today on that court."

"You better not let mom catch you with your feet on that table or she's gonna give all she's got," I said loud enough for my mother to hear.

"Manuel Parker, Sr., you better not have your feet on my table!"

"Did you see my feet on the table, woman?" he shouted back, and then to me he whispered, "Stool pigeon."

I laughed all the way up the stairs. When I reached the bathroom, I could hear the water running in the shower and my brother singing, 'O' by Omarion. I opened the door without knocking.

"Manny, did you talk to Porsha this morning?" I peeped my head in the doorway.

"Yes sir."

"What did she say?"

"She said that Kera told her what time it is; so now she wants a piece of me too. Her and Kera agreed to share me, so I agreed."

"I see it's interrogation time," I said stepping into the bathroom and flushing the toilet, causing the shower's water temperature to feel scalding hot.

"AWW!! OWW!! Stop playing, Ab!" Manny shouted in pain.

"WHAT did Porsha say?" I asked, again.

34

"Man, she just wanted us to hold some good seats for her, Kera and Dymond." The hot water was too much for him to stand.

"Hurry up out the shower, I gotta get in there," I ordered.

"I'll get out when I'm done." This boy loved punishment. So I flushed the toilet again and stepped out the bathroom followed by his screams.

In my room I stripped out of my sweaty clothes, took a quick shower, got dressed in an Akedemic outfit that I bought yesterday and went down to have breakfast with my family. After breakfast, we helped our dad open the store, and then we left for school.

Today the team had a half-day of school courtesy of the 'big game', so after lunch we had to report to the gym for practice; no afternoon classes for us. We went through light warm-ups, with the exception of Jamal. He sat on the bench because of his ripped hamstring. We spent 2 ½ hours working up a sweat before the coach called for a break and everyone hauled up on the bleachers while our coach left the gym to speak to the Principal.

"We ready squad!" Robbie announced, wiping his face with a towel.

"Yea, Newark got drama today; they don't have a shot," Kyle agreed.

"At least if y'all lose, nobody can blame you. I mean… you can't do much without a point guard." Jamal spoke, obviously taking a shot at me. The players turned to me to see if I'd respond.

"We got a point guard, punk! Stop hatin' all your life," Manny spoke up.

"Yeah, and he's better than a 'big mouth' has been," Kyle joined in.

"I'd rather be a 'has been' than a 'never was'," Jamal came back at Kyle. Smirking at me, he said, "I see you got your little girls to fight your battles today."

"Why would I, the starting point guard, even want to fight a battle against the team's mascot? You just make sure you get my towels and Gatorade when I need it! Let me worry about the game," I replied, causing majority of the players to get rowdy, laughing and cheering. It was always two or three that were always on Jamal's side, however, I had more of them siding with me. Clowning around, the coach caught us off guard.

"I see everyone is energized, now, let's get back to work!" All of us moaned and grunted our way back to the court. I winked at Jamal as I passed and poked fun at him, "Have a cup of Gatorade ready for me when I get back." I felt his eyes burning a hole in my back as I walked onto the court.

We practiced for another fifteen minutes before the coach stopped us. He didn't want to overwork us. When we were all seated, he gave us a pep talk.

"Players, today is our day of victory. We've made it too far to lose now! It's either Newark or Howard going to the championship – no other team! I want you guys to ignore the scouts sitting out there, play for the team and win for your team. We will win this game! ARE YOU WITH ME!" Coach gave the shout and we shouted back, "YES!" He continued on with the motivational speech and sent us off to the showers feeling like champions.

We did our routine – showered, got dressed in the locker room for the game. The bus was waiting for us outside.

Kyle, whose locker was next to mine, was on his cell phone trying to talk low, so I wouldn't hear him. When I heard him mention Dymond's name, I started listening. Once he realized I was listening, he told her that he had to go 'cause the coach was calling for the team. He lied.

"Who was that?" I asked him.

"Dang! It was Dymond, if you must know."

"Yea, what happened with you and her yesterday? You never told us," Manny asked from his locker a few feet away.

"That's what I'm saying. Ya'll did come out of the room kind of quick," I added with a devilish grin on my face.

"None of ya' business. Y'all never told me what happened either."

"Oh well, me and Kera did that," Manny said nonchalantly.

"Abdul?" Kyle said, pointing to me.

"Same O, and you, Kyle?" I asked, knowing already that he didn't do anything with Dymond.

"It don't matter, none of us should be doing it anyway."

Manny and me laughed at Kyle, calling him a virgin. Due to horseplay, I didn't notice Jamal approaching. He walked up to me and tossed a full cup of Gatorade directly into my face. Provoking me, he said, "That's the Gatorade you asked for and here's the towel." Then he threw a dirty towel in my face.

Now I knew that if I got into a fight I wouldn't be able to play in the game. And Jamal knew this too, which is why he violated like that. Still knowing all of this, I did what I had to do. He asked for it, so I gave it to him. To put it plain and simple – I made an example of this playa hater! He tried to fight back, but he wasn't much of a match with his injured

37

hamstring. A few players pulled us apart, just as the coach walked in. Now coach didn't actually see us fighting, but with Jamal's nose bleeding like a faucet, we couldn't really get around that.

"What happened?" Coach asked, but no one answered. "We're leaving for the game in a few minutes, but if I don't get some answers, we're not going anywhere," Coach threatened and most of the players started leaking like faucets. They even altered the story a little to make it seem like Jamal threw the first punch.

Everybody – even Jamal's friends – told a story in support of me, because no one wanted to lose their starting Point Guard minutes before the game.

"Parker, I'm going to let you play, but tomorrow, you and Jamal in my office! We're going to straighten this out once and for all. Now all you ladies, on the bus! Double time!" Following Coach's orders, we hustled out to the street and onto the bus, headed for Newark High.

On the bus ride, I was hyped up and nervous. I could also see on everybody's faces that they were all going through a mixture of emotions as I was. Even with the game coming and the fight I had, my mind was managed to find it's way to Porsha's lane. I knew she'd be at the game with Dymond and Kera, rooting yours truly on.

Arriving at Newark High, it was exciting seeing the crowd starting to gather in anticipation of our arrival – their school's competition, arc nemesis, rival, live in the flesh.

The greeting we received were twenty notches below heart warming. They rolled out the red carpet of insults. But we stepped through it all with our heads held high and the swagger we were famous for.

I spotted my boy, Nat posted up in front of the school with a group of his Newark High affiliates. I asked him to meet me there for two reasons. First, to drive my car from Howard, because I was riding the bus; and secondly, so I could remind him on the potential sales at the game. I knew it would be potheads looking for something to celebrate with. I embraced Nat and secretly slipped him a rumpled, small brown, paper bag that I had tucked in my gym bag.

"What's good, Nat?"

"All that can be; how much is in here?"

"Enough, be careful ai'ight. There's going to be adults, parents and teachers in the stands," I warned.

"I got this, Abdul. You focus on scoring 20 points, plus."

"You mean 30 points, plus," I corrected him.

"Yea, that too. What happened to your lip? It looks a little swollen," Nat inquired.

"You should see the other guy," I replied, winking at Nat.

"Who's the other guy?" Nat was looking to start some trouble... or should I say finish it!

"Forget about it, playa. I'll see you after the game." I caught up with my teammates. After we changed, Manny prepared our water bottles on the visitor's bench. Minutes later, we were warming up; as were our opponents. The cheerleaders were also warming up in their little skirts, distracting us. The bleachers were jammed packed. Except, I didn't see Porsha, Kera or Dymond. Manny was waiting for them to arrive, even, holding their seats. I was too busy profiling for the girls who where calling my name. I had to be the number one catch.

I visually searched the stands. I located my parents and seated behind them were Uncle Mark and his wife, Shelley. They waved and I waved back. What my eyes saw next was rewarding. I peeped Porsha, Kera and Dymond gliding through the gym, dressed in their best, looking like divas. I pretended not to see them and acknowledged as many shorties as possible, just to get Porsha jealous. And, it was evident in her angry expression that it was working. Several scouts seated in the first row also caught my attention. I didn't know who was with what college, but knowing they were there was enough. Before the game started, the announcer broadcasted everyone's names. When he announced my name, the immediate rush of both cheers and boo's from the stands were enough to make me know I was 'the man'. I felt like I was soaring high. Regardless of what happened, I'd always remember this moment; it was my moment – a moment to remember.

At tip off, I found myself face-to-face with "Devee Ice, Newark's point guard. Dev was known for making anyone guarding him look retarded. I knew I had to bring my 'A' game today. Dev and me were both positioned to get the jump ball as soon as the ref tossed it up the center. For those few seconds, nothing in the world existed for me but the basketball that the ref was holding. I thought to myself, *'Go ahead, ref toss that ball. I'm getting that, that's me. This is our game, this is our day... 30 plus points, Howard bay-bee!'* The ref blew his whistle and tossed up the ball. Dev made brief eye contact with me, then we both took to the air like eagles with one objective – get the tip ball from the center player!

Chapter Six

Final score: 83 visitors, 57 home Howard crushed Newark High! And no doubt, I managed to pull off my 30 points, 36 to be exact, added with my 12 assists and 10 rebounds. I had a triple double and the scouts were busy taking notes. The crowd was louder than I ever heard and we were celebrating on the court causing them to get louder. My brother started shouting our team's anthem. We joined in the chant along with our fans.

"Get back, get back, you don't know us like that!"

After the game, I spoke with my parents, Uncle Mark and Aunt Shelley. They congratulated me on a spectacular game. I checked Nat for my cash, went to get dressed and later, met up with Porsha, Kera and Dymond at my car. I hugged Porsha and kissed her cheek, as she turned her face away from me, pretending to be madder than she actually was. Still holding her, "That's all I get after scoring 36 points for you?"

"No, you scored one point for me; the other 35 points were for the thirty-five girls you were all geeked about and winking at." Pointing towards females in the standing around, she scowled, "There's a few of your fans over there, go get your kisses from them!"

"Oh! Now that I've given you my body, you wanna pass me off like some property. I've never felt so used – so violated – so cheap!" I joked, acting dramatic. Porsha had to laugh at my antics, dropping her façade of anger. We leaned against my car hugged up, with Manny and Kera; Kyle and Dymond; Nat and some girl, I didn't know were all doing the same – putting their mack down! I'd offered the girls a ride, but they declined. Dymond had already called her aunt to come pick them up. It was cool outside, so we hung out for about a half hour back inside the gym. Then Dymond, Kera and Porsha began tapping each other, signaling one another to look towards the gym doors. I looked and saw two women walking towards us, one of them crying hysterically. The one crying was calling Dymond's name and Dymond began to cry. I didn't know what was going on, cause all the girls started crying, and we just stood around looking stupid trying to figure out what was going on. I caught bits and pieces of the conversation between the girls the two women. I learned that some woman named, Melody, who I assumed was Dymond's mother, was in a bad car accident and they didn't know if she was going to make it. From that point, things got real emotional. Dymond fell to the floor screaming something that I couldn't make out. Porsha and Kera also became distraught. Me, Manny and Kyle tried to comfort the girls. Then, we walked with them to the car. Before they drove off to the hospital, I whispered to Porsha to call me.

After all of that, I really didn't feel much like celebrating. But Manny and Kyle wanted to go this post-game party that Howard students were having. I agreed to drop them off at the party and told them they'd have to get rides home. But of course, I wound up staying with them at the party when I seen how live it was. It was the jump-off! I had big fun!

42

When we finally left the party it was after midnight. I was exhausted from all the physical activity. I'd also talked with a senior named, Brittany that I hadn't paid much attention to before. With Porsha preoccupied, Brittany kept me company. I copped her number but didn't intend on using it. She was a pretty brown fine female. I could tell she wore a weave though. But it fit her well!

Back at home, in my bedroom, I got undressed and jumped into bed sweaty and all, when my cell phone began to vibrate on my nightstand. I checked my alarm clock and saw it was 12:42 am. I answered. It was Porsha. Her voice was raspy, as if she'd been crying all night.

"Hey baby."

"Porsha, how are you?" I was truly concerned, but feeling a bit guilty about hanging out with Brittany all night.

"I'm good; sorry to call you so late…"she apologized, sounding unsure if I was willing to talk.

"Don't worry about it, Porsha. You know I'm here for you whenever you need me. How's your aunt?"

"We don't know yet, she's in critical condition. I don't know what I'll do if she doesn't pull through."

"Don't think like that, Porsha. She's going to be alright. How's Dymond taking this? I know it must be hard on her."

"She's taking it hard. She's right here sleeping next to Kera."

"Where are you right now?"

"We're still in the hospital." I thought to myself that they've been in the hospital all this time and we were out partying while they've been in the emergency room. I felt real bad for a moment.

"When are you going home?"

43

"In the morning, why?"

"I'll stop by to spend some time with you. I have to go by the projects to pick up something. I'll be by after I take care of that."

"I know what you're going to do. Pick me up first, I'll go with you." She said this knowing that I was going by the projects to buy some supply 'cause I had sold out.

"Naa, don't worry about it; you chill. I'll be by afterwards. You have more important things to worry about."

"Abdul, you need somebody to watch your back; I'm coming with you. What time are you going?" she insisted.

"At 1:00 pm."

"Come get me," Porsha persisted.

"Alright."

"Promise, Abdul!"

"I promise."

"Alright, Abdul; I'm gonna let you get some sleep."

"I hope your aunt gets better. Tell Dymond that I'm sorry about what happened," I replied.

"Will do. Goodnight, baby."

"Goodnight."

Chapter Seven

The next day I didn't wake up 'til a lil' after eleven. My house was empty. I knew my parents and Manny were downstairs in the store. I quickly showered and got dressed in a T-shirt, some G-Unit sweatpants and G-Unit sneaks. I grabbed something to eat and lingered around the house doing this and that until the time neared one o'clock. I called my man, Dice in the PJ's (projects), to make sure everything was still a go. He confirmed that he had what I needed and he was waiting on me. Then I called Porsha and told her to be ready; I'd be by to scoop her in ten minutes. I stopped by the store on the way out.

"Well, if it isn't Kobe Bryant! Good morning," my dad greeted me from behind the counter.

"Hey dad, mom and lil' sis," I joked, smacking Manny on the back of his head.

"Don't 'hey mom' me; come over here and give me some sugar." My mom's pride was written all over her face, as I walked over and gave her a hug and a kiss.

"We were all proud of you last night, son." My dad beamed, "Even your little sister, Manny," he smiled.

"Alright, alright! Enough with the 'little sister' joke," Manny cut in.

"Where are you headed, Chris?" my mom asked.

"To go spend some time with Porsha. Her aunt was in a serious car accident last night." I wasn't completely lying yet; I just wasn't telling the whole truth.

"Is her aunt's name Melody?"

"Yea, how'd you know that?"

"I read it in the paper this morning; her car flipped over several times. How is she?" Mom inquired.

"She's in critical condition," I responded.

"Tell Porsha, we'll keep her aunt in our prayers," mom said.

"Alright, mom. I'll see you guys later." With those last words I left out the store, not wanting to delay my plan any longer.

When I arrived in my hooptie to pick Porsha up, she was home alone. Her face looked worn; her eyes were red and puffy. I wasn't sure if it was from lack or sleep or crying. She climbed into the passenger's seat and we headed out to the projects.

"Has your aunt's condition changed?" I asked. We were riding with the music turned off.

"No, she's still on critical watch. Thanks for asking."

"When are you going back to the hospital?"

"At 5:00 this evening, my mom and me are meeting Dymond and her Dad out there."

"I'm going with you, if that's okay," I offered.

"I'm not to sure about that. Uncle Tone don't play that boyfriend/girlfriend stuff."

We pulled up a few blocks away from Dice's building. I parked in a position where we could see his building from

46

the car. Before stuffing my money down into my sweatpants, I decided to count it again to make sure it was the correct amount.

"Porsha, I need you to stay in the car and watch my back from here, okay?"

"Yeah, what do you want me to do?"

"You see that building over there?"

"Yes."

"That's where I'm meeting him at. If you see anything funny – anything at all, you beep the horn. But don't get out of the car regardless of what happens," I instructed her.

"I got you."

I gave her a pound for being my down chick and got out of the car, leaving it running, telling her to get in the driver's seat. As I neared the building, I looked around scanning the area. There were a few people hanging around and some going about their business, but overall everything appeared normal. When I reached Dice's building, two guys stepped out dressed in jeans and scuffed up Timberland boots. Both men appeared to be in their early twenties and one was carrying a black duffle bag.

"Yo! My man, you here to see Dice?" the one with the black duffle bag interrogated.

"Why? What's it to you?"

"We work for him. He had to step out to handle some other business. We got your stuff right here in the bag." He cut his eyes to his boy. "Where's the money?" the same guy said, gesturing towards the bag in his hand.

I really didn't like this; it seemed shady. He could've mentioned this to me. I was going to turn and keep it moving, but I needed my supply to make money, and I didn't drive over here for nothing.

47

Platinum Teen Series

"Let me see what's in the bag," I told them. They exchanged a look and the one without the bag nodded his approval. The other man opened the bag and showed me the contents. Everything seemed to be there, so I pulled the money from my pocket. As I handed the man the money, the other handed me the bag. I stood by examining the bag's contents, while the other man counted the money. After seeing the product was right, I closed the bag and said, "Yo, tell Dice..." HONK! HONK! HONK! My train of thought was interrupted by the sound of a car horn... my car horn!

I turned in time to see an undercover cop rushing towards me. Then I felt the man (that I thought was down) with the money grab me by my t-shirt and yelled, "Police! You're under arrest!" By reflex, I elbowed in the stomach and clutched the duffle bag and haul-tailed. When the other lunged towards me, I threw the bag in his face and jetted (took off running). It seemed like cops were coming from everywhere, chasing me down. I had no intentions of getting caught. I couldn't risk my scholarship! Dipping and dodging, cutting corners and jumping fences as I ran – I just couldn't seem to lose them! As I made it toward the street the car was parked on, the car was gone! I began to slow down, running out of steam. The police were gaining on me; I just knew I was done. To my surprise, here come my car jumping the curb and screeching to a stop three feet in front of me. It was Porsha; she said she had my back and she meant it. She pushed the passenger door open and shouted, "COME ON AB!" I dove inside my car, yelling, "GO!! GO!! GO!!!" She pulled off quickly, side swiping a parked car as she drove off the sidewalk going back into the street. We raced down the street with police cars in pursuit. Unexpectedly, an unmarked police car cut us off, blocking the street up ahead of us. Porsha panicked and cut the wheel to the left hard. She jumped the curb again, hitting a fire hydrant on an angle that caused the car to flip over. We landed upside down and slid about ten feet on the car's roof, coming to a hard stop when we bumped into a parked car. Turning to see Porsha, I blacked out....

Chapter Eight

I woke up on a hard bench in a cold cell. I wasn't sure where I was or how I got there; the past events to me were fuzzy. My head was hurting with extreme pain. Touching my forehead, I discovered a large tender lump. Then it came back to me – I remembered bumping my head on the dashboard when we hit the fire hydrant and flipped over. That's when I realized where I was – I was in jail. Looking around, the cell was small, dully painted, with two small benches and had an open-for-all-to-see toilet. On the other bench, a young teenager no older than sixteen was sleeping. I stood carefully and walked to the front of the cell where the bars allowed me to look out into the corridor. Not seeing anyone out there, I called out, "Hey, Officer! Anybody out there?" No one answered. The feeling of being watched alerted my senses. I turned and found the other kid no longer sleeping, but sitting on his bench watching me. He appeared to be about my height, smaller in build, dark-skinned with locks that were shoulder length.

"Call for the Turn Key, he'll come see what you want," he informed me.

"Call for *what*?" I asked him, confused.

"Just yell, Turn-Key," he spoke slowly.

"Turn Key!" I shouted. "Turn Key!"

"What do you want?" a deep voice came from down the corridor out of our sight.

"Come down here and find out!" the kid on the bench shouted disrespectfully. "You hear him calling you!"

Walking down the hallway corridor was a tall, thick white man with a blonde crew cut dressed in a blue police uniform, looking pissed off to the max.

Scornfully scrutinizing me, "I see sleeping beauty has awakened. It seems like high speed police chases don't agree with you," he said, gesturing to the lump on my forehead. "An you," he pointed to the other kid, "Keep your fat lips quiet!"

"Where's Porsha; is she alright?" I asked like her knew her.

"You must be talking about your little get-away driver. Her mother came to pick her up about two hours ago," the police officer told me.

"Well, I want my parents to come and get me."

"They were already here. There's one problem," he said with a smirk on his face. "Your parents, well, they said this experience should teach you a lesson." His same arrogant smirk made it obvious that he enjoyed his status while giving me bad news.

"Well, how much is my bail?"

"You don't have one; you go before the judge tomorrow," he told me.

"So, I'll have to stay here 'til tomorrow?"

"Welcome to the life of crime," he sarcastically said, walking away.

"Well, can I get something to eat?" My stomach was filled with hunger pains.

"Chow time's in a little bit over an hour - you'll have to wait," was the last thing he said, before disappearing from my view.

"He's an idiot. What's your name?" the kid on the bench asked.

"Abdul, what's yours?"

"They call me Fabian. What they get you for, Abdul?"

"I think my peeps set me up. I was going to re-up and the cops were waiting for me. It turned into a high-speed chase. My girl crashed into a fire hydrant and here I am. How about you?"

"I got a body."

"You got a *what*?" I wasn't sure if I'd heard him correctly.

"A body... a murder charge. I slumped this trick for disrespecting my set," he said. This guy, my age, was telling me he was a murderer.

"Do you bang?"

"Yea, 9-Tray Blood. What set you claim?" he said, making several signs with his fingers.

"Oh, I don't bang. Why did you... you know?" I asked, not wanting to say it.

"He was a crab," he snuffed. Then he realized I didn't understand. "...a crip, rollin' 60's. He was flaggin' and stackin' on my set, so I ate his food." To translate: he said the other guy was a member of the Crips and was wearing his blue scarf and making gang signs with his hands – so he killed him. I wasn't completely disconnected or sheltered from the streets; so I knew, like most kids my age, that gang banging was a dangerous life. But sitting there in that cell listening to Fabian, I couldn't swallow the idea of someone being murdered for such trivial reasons.

"How old was he?"

"About my age or younger."

"How old are you?" He had me curious now.

"I turned sixteen last week," answering like it was the same age as thirty-one. Here was a kid my little brother's age, locked up for killing another kid *also* my brother's age. Unbelievable, yet it was reality.

"Your parents let you bang? I mean my parents would be dead set against it if I mentioned banging around them."

"My set is my parents; my parents were killed in a drug raid by the police. They didn't want to go to jail, so they choose death. That was gangsta. I've been on my own ever since until I joined my set. Now they're my family," Fabian explained and I'm thinking what is gangsta about choosing death that was pure stupidity.

"No offense, but I couldn't choose death over a drug charge. I'd rather go to jail for a while and have chance to start over."

"But you did choose death over a drug charge. You and your girl, just like my mother and father," he said.

"What are you talking about? Neither one of us is dead." I didn't quite understand what he was getting at.

"You were lucky – or unlucky, depending how you look at it."

"What?"

"Think about it, Abdul. You're not alive by choice you're alive by luck. You and your girl could've both been killed in that high-speed chase; either by a crash or the cops could've shot and killed you both. You could've surrendered, but you chose death," he summarized with the logic and wisdom of an old man.

Fabian was right, I hadn't thought about it like that. I really hadn't thought about it at all. I changed the subject, "You ever think about quitting?"

"Quitting what?" he replied.

"You know… gang banging," I said.

"Why?" he asked, seeming oblivious to the risks of banging.

"There are a lot of reasons… but just let's say what happens if you get shot?" I asked, thinking I was making a good point. He pulled up his shirt, showing a massive scar running up from his belly button to his upper chest. Someone had sliced his skin tissue terribly. He began pointing to numerous bullet wounds, seven in total.

"See, I've already been shot; and my set rode out for me. Let's just say that kid won't be shooting anymore of the homies," Fabian bragged and was proudly wearing his bullet wounds and scars as a badge of honor. The more I looked at him, the more I envisioned my brother and I couldn't bear the thought of Manny laying in the streets with seven bullet holes in his chest or cut up in pieces like a pizza.

"Why would you wanna live like that?"

"Why would you?" Fabian was serious.

"What? I'm not living like that."

"Yeah, you are. Why would you want to live my life?"

"I don't. I live with my parents, go to school everyday, get good grades, I'm on the school's basketball team and hopefully I'm about to get a basketball scholarship to college," I explained.

"Yet and still, here you are sitting in a jail cell with me…so, I ask you again, if you have all of that going for you, why would you throw all of it away to live my life?"

"I… uhh…" I was stuck on stupid.

54

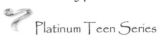

THE AB-SOLUTE TRUTH   Juwell & Precious

"I mean I don't have none of that… I gangbang 'cause it's all I know. I can't even read or write. If I don't stick with my set, I can't survive. I can't sell drugs without them. If I don't sell drugs, I don't eat at night. Do you know what it feels like to be homeless and hungry not knowing when the next meal is coming? I ride with my set because they ride for me. We real heavy in Cali, but they – the riders (judges) called themselves breaking us up. They sent me out here for Boot Camp. Even that didn't help, I got into it with a square dude and here I am hoping I can get back to my set to be with my family. You don't have an excuse Abdul." His conversation shut my mouth and opened my eyes. He was telling nothing but the truth. I knew what I was doing was wrong. My Uncle Mark even warned me to stop. But, it took this sixteen year old gangbanger to show me the error of my ways. Then I began to realize that ending up in this jail cell was an endorsement telling Manny that it was okay for him to live the same way. I could be the cause of my brother turning out like Fabian and me. I also exposed Porsha to danger. I was not only jeopardizing myself, but others in my circle. It was time for me to re-evaluate my life and put my priorities in perspective. I stayed up most of the night talking to Fabian and learning to appreciate the hand I've been dealt, because there was always some else out there less fortunate.

The next afternoon, I was ushered to court wearing handcuffs and leg irons. When I entered the courtroom, I saw my mother, father, Manny and Uncle Mark seated in the front row talking to a heavyset, black woman with long hair. Despite the tears in her eyes, my mother managed to smile and wave to me. Seeing her like this, I knew I had hurt her, as well as my father. Uncle Mark wouldn't even look at me; I could imagine how he must have felt. He was probably blaming himself, being that he knew about it. My name was called and a cop guided me to a small podium where the woman, who had talked with my parents, came and stood by my side. She introduced herself to me, "Mr. Christopher Parker, I'm your attorney, Ms. Melissa Pearch."

"Who hired you, my parents?"

"No, sir. I'm court appointed. Today is just your arraignment, you'll enter your guilty or not guilty plea and the judge will set your bail. I'd advise that you plead not guilty. I'll work on getting you a reasonable bail," she instructed me.

"What's a reasonable bail?"

"Twenty-five hundred unsecured," she said so casually, you'd think she said twenty-five dollars.

"How much? That's not reasonable," I argued. I didn't understand the bail process, but I knew my parents couldn't afford that. Fabian already told me that if I couldn't make bail, I'd be going over to the juvenile jail until I got out. The judge started reading off my charges, more so to himself. My lawyer started arguing with a man who turned out to be the prosecutor. The prosecutor was pushing for a $5,000 bail; my lawyer was opposing with a $2,500 unsecured bond, and it sounded like the prosecutor was winning. After considering both arguments, the judge decided to be lenient on me. Being that I was a good student, my parents were upstanding citizens in the community and the fact that I'd never been in trouble – he set my bail at $1,000 secured bond. Which meant, I went to jail that night. For me to get out of jail, my parents had to pay $1000.00.

"Your Honor, I move for a bail reduction and request that Mr. Parker be released today in the custody of his parents," Ms. Pearch was straightforward with the female judge.

"Denied," the judge said.

"Your Honor, my client's parents can't afford to pay the bond. We see no reason for the defendant to remain in jail unnecessarily," Ms. Pearch argued.

"You see no reason for him to remain in jail? Ms. Pearch, I see plenty of reasons. The defendant is a drug dealer who assaulted two police detectives, resisted arrest, took them on a high speed chase through a residential community with another minor behind the wheel – all of which, he's only receiving probation for. So... Ms. Pearch, whether or not he makes bail isn't one of my concerns.

Ms. Pearch leaned in and said, "Sorry, Mr. Parker."

I looked back at my family; my mother was crying and my father was trying to comfort her. Porsha was also crying; even Manny was looking as if he was about to burst into tears.

Chapter Nine

I spent seven days in the juvenile facility before I was allowed my first visit. My family showed up and it was an emotional moment. My mother was there along with my father, Manny and Uncle Mark. Mom was crying and hugging on me as if I were dying. Even my dad looked as if he were about to cry. My brother kept looking around in amazement like he was a tourist in New York City.

We were seated at table large enough for us all.

"How are you holding up, son?" Dad asked.

"Yea, do you need anything, Ab?" Manny chimed in.

"Yes, to get outta here!"

"Now look, Chris we're not going to preach to you; at least I'm not. But you need to know that $1000 is hard to come by for someone that chose to get in trouble!"

"I know mom."

"Abdul, you go back to court in a few days for a bail reduction. We're going to try to get you out of here on your next court date. Keep your nose clean until then," Uncle Mark instructed.

"Thanks a lot, Uncle Mark; I don't know how I could repay you."

"Well, I do," he retorted, while cutting his eye at my mother as a kind of signal for something. My mother reached into her purse and retrieved an envelope handing it to me. The envelope, which had already been opened, was from the University of Syracuse. Stunned and heart racing, I looked up at my family, who waiting on my response. I removed the letter in haste and read it just as fast. It was an offer for a full basketball scholarship, if I wished to attend their university. *If I wish to attend,* they made it sound like it was a privilege for them to have me attend.

Uncle Mark got right to the point. "You're going to pay me back by attending college and making all of us proud." I agreed happily and the visit lighted up. I explained what happened and how I got locked up. Everyone told me how stupid I was, except Manny. His stupid butt said, "Man, that was gangsta!" My parents and Uncle Mark began talking amongst themselves, allowing me time to talk to him.

"What's been going on out there?"

He excitedly whispered on the low, "Man, everybody at schools been talking! I heard so many different stories; none like what you told."

"Who's telling the stories?" I asked.

"Everybody!"

"Where's it coming from?"

"Who knows, but I do know you've created a celebrity," he pulled his lips in tightly. Long and as serious as I could look him in his eyes, I warned him, "This ain't nothing to be proud of; I'm not a celebrity."

"I'm not talking about you; I'm talking about Porsha," he corrected me. At the mention of Porsha, my heart began racing. I hadn't seen her seen the court appearance.

"What do you mean she's a celebrity? I hope she's not out there bragging about what happened."

"Man, everyday somebody is giving her props, treating her like she's an action hero. She's even been hanging around different people since you've been in here, like - " Manny's voice trailed off like he does when he's hiding something from me.

"Different people like who?" I asked firmly.

"Jamal and his boys," he informed me, reluctantly. My girl was hanging around with my enemy while I sat and rot in jail. That little news really, really upset me; but I didn't want to show it.

"Does she know that you saw her with them?"

"Yea, you know me... I said something to both of them about it."

"What did you say to them?"

"I told Jamal to enjoy my brother's leftovers," that's all.

"What did she say about that?"

"She cursed me out."

"What did Jamal say?"

"Something slick, I can't remember. Whatever it was, I was gonna bust his lip, but Kyle and Nat broke it up before I could get at him."

"Man, I don't care. I received a letter from the girl Brittany anyway. She's all on my jock." I gripped my chin, "Leave that cat Jamal alone, Manny; Porsha too. Anyway, what have you been up to?" I switched up to hide how I was truly feeling.

"I've been chillin', doing me. How about you? What's it like in here?" he asked me in wide-eyed fascination. I could tell that he really wanted to be in there just to see what it was like. So, I gave him the real.

"You want real? A kid was sexually violated, beat and busted up last night. Not to mention that you can't do anything without the staff's permission and that's not cool when you need to drop a load. They speak to us rudely and most times treat us wrong. Most of the dudes in here don't care if they live or die; so, if you don't feel the same way, you don't fit it." The more I told him about the joint, the less he seemed fascinated. I went on to explain to him that the only reason I was exempt from most of the daily dramas in jail was because I had a guardian angel named, Fabian. Fabian was moved off my unit, but he still had my back. He was on a unit with the worst of the worst – juveniles charged as adults, waiting to be transferred. He let other know I was bulletproof; which meant that I was untouchable and nothing was to happen to me while I was there.

Our visit was over and I was confident that when my little brother left, any interests he had about jail, he left them behind when he departed. It was a painful ordeal to watch my family walk out that door. But the worst part was the agony and suffering in my mother's eyes; it was killing her, tearing her apart, breaking her heart to see her baby caged and held hostage in a place like this. I could tell she was puzzled and wondered where she went wrong. I wanted to scream out to her that this was my fault and not to take the blame. But the heavy doors slammed shut behind them with a cold, uncompromising feeling of finality. That night, secretly, I cried without caring about what the other guys thought of me.

Chapter Ten

The days came and went and I maneuvered through the minefields of jail life, until the following week when I was finally taken back to court. When I entered the courtroom, I saw my family seated in the same place and Porsha, a row behind them. When we made eye contact, she blew me a kiss and mouthed the words, "*I love you.*" I wanted to smile at her, but I didn't. I needed to keep a straight face.

Ms. Pearch, my attorney, met me at the doors and walked with me to our seats at the defense table. Once we were seated, she began to explain things to me in a low voice.

"Mr. Parker, how are you this morning?"

"I'm alright." I answered detached from everything, except for getting out of jail.

"I've negotiated an acceptable deal. They are willing to settle your case, drop the charges that would prohibit you from attending college, drop the bail, and have you report to Probation for a period of 6 months. You need to thank God for your coach and that scholarship letter, do you understand?"

"Yes, ma'am," I complied.

"The conditions of your probation state that you must attend college. This doesn't happen often, trust me!"

"I understand."

"So, you need to take full advantage of this. Also, Probation Officer Mark Stone has agreed to make sure you follow through," she expounded. "But," she began to hesitate, "the judge has to agree to the terms that the prosecutor and I negotiated."

"What do you think she'll do?" I asked her worried.

"I can't say for sure, but with your clean record, the college scholarship and Mr. Stone's influence behind you, your chances are good."

"So, when will I be getting out?"

"Hopefully, later on today."

When my name was called, I walked up to the podium with Ms. Pearch and faced Judge Alford the woman who would decide my fate. I was so disappointed in myself for doing something so stupid that could have ruined my life. All for what?... some sneaks, a few outfits and to treat my girl from time to time? I had missed the championship game. Even though our team won the championship, it wasn't the same without me playing.

"Mr. Christopher Parker, do you understand the severity of your crimes?"

"Yes, your honor," I humbly replied.

"And the state has agreed to the defendant receiving six months of probation in which, his charges will be dropped if he complies with attending Syracuse University?"

"Yes, your honor," the prosecutor answered.

"And... um... Probation Officer Mr. Mark Stone," the judge spoke visually searching the courtroom, "is he here today?" Uncle Mark stood up, "Yes, your Honor."

"Would you please step forward?"

Uncle Mark walked up front to where I stood with Ms. Pearch and took his place at my side.

"Mr. Stone, have you agreed to supervise the defendant?"

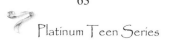

"Yes, your Honor; I have," he confirmed.

Peering over her humongous desk, Judge Alford asked me, "Young man, do you realize you have a lot of good people on your side? This is the first time I've ever accepted a deal such as this. You better not make me regret this!"

"Yes, your Honor," I replied earnestly. She in turn fixed her eyes on me, staring at me intensely and thoughtfully for several seconds. I could tell she was contemplating on whether or not she should apply her signature to the plea. My future and life was solely in her hands. My heart pounded in my chest with the force of thunder in the sky on a stormy night.

"Mr. Parker," the Judge Alford began, "I'm going to accept these terms, but let me tell you something..." she was forcefully staring at me again, "...you will go to college. You will report to Mr. Stone weekly, who will keep us up on your progress. Also, I'm ordering you to attend an Anger Management class to cool that temper of yours down! If you violate any of your conditions or land in any courtroom again for any reason, I promise you that you'll be sorry that you ever met me, understood?"

"Yes, Judge Alford; I understand," I said quickly before she could bang the gavel. I was headed back to gather my things for release!

"PARKER!" Snapping me out of my thoughts was the voice of an officer calling out my name. I got up and approached the gate, ready to go back over to jail. Soon as we got there, they were ready to release me.

A guard approached carrying a card with my picture on it. He asked, "You're Parker?"

"Yes," I said.

The officer looked from me to the picture and back to me. "Parker, you're out," he said. "Don't come back, ya' here me."

I assured him, "I'm not!"

Chapter Eleven

Since I'd been home, for some reason, everything seemed different. Then it hit me like a ton of bricks; something did change – me. Nothing was different; I just looked at things differently. Especially, not to take anything for granted. The first day of my liberation from prison life, expressed my gratitude to my parents, Uncle Mark, and Coach.

During the first few weeks that I was out, I was put on house arrest. Not by the courts, the jail or by the judge. I was on the worst house arrest of all; I was on mom and dad's house arrest. Yea, I know I'm not the only one who's experienced it. That's right; my schedule consisted of school, time for basketball, working in my parent's store and in the house. Grounded wasn't the word for what I was going through; they were on the heels of my ankles! Manny even got more than I did. I couldn't complain though, it was better than jail.

My father drove me to the police pound were my car was being held. We got a court order for them to release it. When I saw my car, I was amazed at the damage. I didn't remember seeing my baby that battered and beaten after the accident. Then again, I didn't remember too much of anything after the accident. I had to pay $460, for the time my car was impounded. Not to mention whatever I'd be charged for repairs. My dad offered to pay the police pound fees, if I could find an affordable auto body shop to come and tow my car for repairs. The next day I talked to my boy, Nat about my car, because his father owned a car shop. Nat's dad agreed to fix my car for $300, which was an excellent deal. After that, I felt obligated to pick Nat up for school in the mornings and drop him off in the afternoons to show my appreciation. It became routine to pack Manny and Nat into my car after school. Porsha and me still hadn't had that one on one conversation about the rumors. But this particular afternoon, I was chillin' with my boys so I was pressed to chat about that.

"Yo, Nat? I thought you wanted to be a ball player? How come you never tried out?" Even though Manny wasn't a member himself, he was sure Nat wanted to be down with the team.

"For real, Nat; you might as well. You were at every game or practice that we ever had more than the cheerleaders," I joined in.

"I don't play basketball; I play cheerleaders. That's why I'm always at practice."

"I second that; you do get all the cheerleaders I don't want or that I've already had," Manny said popping his collar and brushing off his shoulder.

"Yea, right Manny. You can't do nothing without Kera finding out," Nat defended.

"Man, she don't run me. I ain't Ab and she ain't Porsha," he replied, taking a shot at my neck to see if I'd tense up.

"You know the chain of command; I control Porsha, she controls Kera and Kera controls you. So, respect your elders, son," I checked Manny.

67

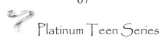

"Yea, respect your superiors young boy!" Nat cut in.

"Yo, Nat seriously, I need $50. I'll pay you back," Manny said.

"When... the 33rd of Never-ary? I know I'm not getting it back." Then Nat pulled out a wad of money from his pockets. He peeled of two twenties and a ten dollar bill, handing it to Manny. I thought Nat would be smart enough to leave that stuff alone from my experiences, but I see from his cash flow he hadn't. Since I got arrested, I hadn't come near anything illegal.

"Nat, where did you get all that money from," I asked him, watching him out of the corner of my eye as I drove.

"Where do you think I got it from?" Nat smirked, shoving the money back into his pocket.

"I know you're not still hustling?" They made an example out of me already, so I couldn't figure out why Nat would be stupid enough to keep hustling.

"Of course I'm still hustling. The game don't stop just 'cause you got knocked."

"Look man, I'm not gonna preach to you about it, 'cause I used to do it. But trust me, you don't want to end up where I've been," I told him from the heart.

"Man, just 'cause the cops shook you don't mean the world stops turning. Don't knock my hustle and I won't knock yours," he spat.

"I won't knock your hustle and I won't help you with it either. I can't have nothing to do with it. But I will give you a word of advice, if you dealing with my old connect, it won't be long before you end up in jail!"

"Ab, I don't need that snitch, my people look out for me. Check this out – look." Nat unzipped his backpack, holding it open showing me his plastic bags of product. I

68

almost lost my mind. I smashed on the breaks, bringing the car to a screeching halt.

"FOOL!! IS YOU *CRAZY!* I KNOW YOU AIN'T SITTIN' UP HERE IN MY RIDE WITH DRUGS!"

"Calm down, Ab! It's just a little weed!" As if that would defuse my anger.

"You bumped your head! I'm fresh out of Juvie Hall on 6 months probation, nut!... driving in the SAME car I got caught in. How stupid could you be?" I wanted to haul off and punch him in his grill (face). If I had gotten pulled over, just on a traffic violation, the judge would've thrown the book at me; and Uncle Mark and my parents would've allowed it, and rightfully so.

"Ay, Manny tell this dude to slow his role; he's over-reacting." Nat was looking at Manny for support, but Manny didn't say a thing. He knew I was on the verge of hurting something, or someone.

"Nat, check this out playa... you know I love you like a brother, but as long as you're selling weed or any other drugs, I can't deal with you anymore, whatsoever, and you can't ride with me with that bag of weed."

Nat was speechless, sitting there staring blankly ahead out the car window. "You want me to get out *right now, right here?*" he asked, bewildered.

"Yea, man. It's nothing personal; I just can't afford the risk. I have too much to lose at this stage in my life and that's not the route I wanna take," unbending and unyielding I confessed to him.

"I gotta respect that; you're still my people. Manny, I'll catch up with you later. Holla." Nat stepped out the car, knowing this was a decision I had to maintain. As we pulled off, I watched Manny in the rearview mirror. I'm glad he was

69

there to witness that; I wanted him to recognize that nobody was worth throwing away your future. No matter how much you valued a friend, a true friend would only want what's best for you. Anything less, is less than a friend!

"Manny, I don't want you hanging around Nat. He's headed where I left." I had only completed three sessions on Anger Management and I was being tested already.

"I'm way ahead of you, bro'," Manny sprung back, making me proud of his response. We had to distance ourselves from anyone who was poison to us.

I'd been communicating with Porsha scarcely since I'd been out. We talked at school and over the phone, but we couldn't hang out much due to my mom and pop's keeping me on house arrest. Porsha understood and told me she'd wait patiently for me. Staying on point, I asked my parents for leniency. I needed to get out of the house. They agreed, but reminded me of my curfew. I couldn't remember the last time I had a curfew to make, but I had no choice, I didn't beef (argue). I called Porsha to ask her out to a movie; she quickly accepted. I picked her up outside her house early for two reasons: first, cause we didn't have much time due to my curfew and secondly, I didn't want to run into her mother, who I knew still blamed me for getting her baby girl locked up. We went to a movie and then out to dinner at a soul food spot I knew about. I ordered the oxtails, beans, rice and cabbage. While Porsha had the fried chicken, rice, black-eyed peas and corn on the cob. We choose to sit at the window to enjoy our meals and each other's company.

"I'm happy to see that mommy and daddy finally let the little baby out the crib to come out and play," Porsha teased.

"Oh, I see you got jokes today."

70

"We haven't been out in a long time, what do you expect?"

"It hasn't been that long."

"Yes, it has. The last time we spent any quality time together, our date ended upside down in your car."

"Don't remind me, please."

"How could you forget?"

"I can't. Let me ask you something that's been on my mind for a minute... what made you come to my rescue?"

"You don't know?"

"Enlighten me," I probed.

"It's simple – love." Porsha reached across the table, placing her soft, manicured hands on top of mine. We caught each other's eye and held on for several seconds, communicating without words.

"Although that was sweet, your act of saving me could have been deadly. Thank you for looking out, but don't ever try that again."

"I'm know, but I was willing to risk my life for you." The moment was heart warming, but I had to spoil it.

"Don't you ever let me hear you say that again! Nobody is worth risking your life for!" There was more that I had to get off my chest, "Porsha, were you hanging around Jamal and his crew while I was locked up?"

"I knew Manny was gonna tell you and make it sound funny like something was going on," she said defensively. The momentum changed quickly. This put me on alert status.

"What did you expect? He's my brother, but you still didn't answer the question."

"Who else was I supposed to hang with? I mean you were gone."

"How about Kera and Dymond? That's who you've been hanging around with?"

"Neither one of them goes to our school and after school they were always with Manny and Kyle. I wasn't trying to be the 5th wheel."

"Where you involved with Jamal? Tell me the truth!"

"You know better than to ask me or to even think something like that!"

"And you know better than to play another guy close like that, much less my enemy." How could she do this, I thought.

"So, now you care about what other people think, huh?" Porsha had the nerve to wild out on me when she was in the wrong.

"No, I care about what you do behind my back." I regretted it immediately after saying it, but it was too late to take it back. Porsha sat staring at me with tears swelling in her eyes as if I had just backhand slapped her in the face. Then calmly speaking, Porsha made clear, "Look, Abdul I didn't do anything wrong. If this is what you brought me here for, then you can take me home right now."

"I'm sorry, Porsha. I got a lot on my mind and I guess I let dumb school rumors get to me."

"Apology accepted. I know you've been stressing a little. I even heard that you and Nat had a fallout." She was quick to mention that. I guess to jump to another subject.

"I wouldn't say a fallout; I had to cut him off."

"Why, what happened?" she asked.

"Well, he's still selling drugs and he got in my car with it on him. I gotta start staying away from all trouble. Graduation is coming real soon. I can't jeopardize that for nobody," I explained.

Porsha got quiet suddenly, with the saddest look in her eyes; just staring at me as is she were looking through me.

"What did I say?"

"No, it' nothing," she replied dismissively; but I could tell that something was eating her.

"Porsha? What's on your mind?"

"It's just... well... you reminded me that I'm going to lose you again and this time it may be for good." She spoke low and timidly; it was almost a whisper.

"What are you talking about?"

"I heard you got a scholarship to Syracuse University. You'll be leaving after the summer. With all those college girls, what would you want with a high school girl? I mean, you'll be almost done in college before I even graduate," she said.

"It ain't like that Porsha and you know it," I said, trying to reassure her.

"No, I don't. You'll be a grown man and I'll be a little girl. You'll have a bunch of women to choose from, why would you still want me?"

"There's nothing little about you, shortie," I said laughing; then I leaned forward and pinched the baby fat on her side. "Baby, we've been through too much for me to throw it away. I don't want a college girl; I want you.

She smiled and asked, "That's what you say now!"

I smiled back.

Chapter Twelve

Uncle Mark called me and told me to meet him over the Probation office. I met him and went over some paperwork and other formalities, such as drug testing and photographing. He showed me around the office introducing to all of his co-workers, who once were my late brother's co-workers and friends. He took me to the memorial room and showed me my brother's memorial plaque that was signed by the Mayor's office. It all began to set in how wrong it was for me to be here signing up for probation. What a way for me to honor my deceased brother! I felt shamed. I had a lump in my throat as I fought back the tears the entire time I spent in that office, knowing it would've broken Tyrone's heart, if he were still alive. Leaving Uncle Mark's office, I was in a quiet mood of solitude on the way home. Just reflecting on all I've been through and all the mistakes I'd made. I was also contemplating my plans for rectifying my errors and reversing all the negativity I instilled in my baby brother. As he drove, I felt Uncle Mark watching me.

"Hey, Abdul; a penny for your thoughts."

74

"If that offer was a valid one, you'd make me a rich dude," I said.

"It's that deep, huh?"

"Uncle Mark, keep it real... I need to ask you something."

"What's up?"

"Have you ever done anything stupid when you were my age?" Uncle Mark started laughing so, I asked, "What's so funny?"

"Abdul, we all do stupid stuff at your age. We do stupid stuff at my age. It's human nature, we're not perfect."

"For real?"

"Of course, Abdul. Your mistakes don't define who you are; how you bounce back does. Don't think for a second that you're a bad person because you committed a bad act, just recognize where you went wrong and learn from it. Use it to teach someone else. Life is about 2nd chances, Abdul," he explained.

"I just hope none of this reflects on Manny; you know he wants to be the man. I won't be able to look out for him when I go away to school," I sighed worried.

"He'll be alright. He has your parents and me on backup. You don't worry about Manny. You focus on school. College is a big step you know."

"Yea, I know – the parties, the girls, the beer and the booze," I joked.

"And the books! Don't play with me, boy!" He punched me in my arm playfully.

"What are you gonna do about your girlfriend, the getaway driver? The Bonnie to your Clyde, the Christina Milian to Nick Cannon, the Ciara to Bow-wow?" he asked, referring to Porsha.

"What do you mean?"

"You're going away to school, you can't take her with you. You gonna let her go?"

"Naa, that's my girl. I can't let her go."

"Why not? You think that a long distance relationship is going to work?"

"Why shouldn't it?" I asked Uncle Mark.

"I don't know, good luck with that," he said, without looking at me, as if he knew the answer and didn't want to hurt my feelings by telling me right then.

"What are you saying? It won't work out?" I asked him, knowing there was a hidden message in his words and I was determined to get to the bottom of it.

"Think about it, Abdul she's used to being the girlfriend of the 'big man' in school, the famous Abdul, the basketball playing senior, dealing with a freshman. When you leave, she becomes a 'Plain Jane'. You think she won't be looking for another basketball playing senior to replace you?" She doesn't want that attention to die down. It will be on to the next guy to keep her rep up." What he said really got under my skin. In the time I was locked up, she latched onto Jamal just that quickly. Maybe there was some truth to what he was saying, I considered.

Uncle Mark continued, "How about the flip side of the coin? You'll be going to a new school with thousands of pretty young women, all fresh faces. You're going to be on the basketball team, do you have any idea how many girls will be coming at you everyday? Now, you ask yourself will it work. I think you know the answer already." He had me thinking. How could I dispute that? None, of this had I given much thought. There was no doubt in my mind that Porsha was my

76

teenage love. I just began to question would our feelings for each other fade while we're apart.

When we pulled up in front of my parent's store, Uncle Mark got out of the car when I did. I thought he was going to say "hi" to my parents, but I had another thing coming. Approaching me, he instructed, "Abdul, put your hands on the car."

"What?" I thought he was joking.

"I'm not playing, Abdul; do as I say please," he repeated seriously and I complied taken back by his actions.

Uncle Mark quickly pat-frisked me, finding nothing.

"Alright. Tell your parents I send my love." With that, he got back in the car as if nothing happened.

"Uncle Mark! What was that all about?"

"It's called a random 'pat frisk'; get used to it. I have to make sure you're not carrying drugs at anytime."

"Why couldn't you ask me? You don't trust me?"

"I asked you would you stop selling weed a while back; you looked me in the eyes and lied. Trust is something you earn. I love you, but you have to earn my trust back."

Wow! I said to myself, *that lie sure came back to haunt me.*

In my parents' store, I found them hard at work. I joined in and began helping serve the customers. When the store was empty, I explained to them about my visit to the probation building. Shortly before closing time, we received a surprise visit from Porsha, Kera and Dymond.

"What's up Porsha, Kera, and Miss Dymond In The Rough? I asked with warm greetings. My mother asked Dymond about her mother's condition due to her car accident as they stepped inside the store.

"Not Mr., 'Dymond so stuck-up' ain't try'na be nice! I can't believe the lion has a heart." Dymond even made me laugh at that.

"I'm not a cold dude Miss Conceited." Then from nowhere all of them thought they were Remy Ma singing, *"I look too good to be hearing that. I'm conceited, I gotta reason!"* They were swaying from side to side, interrupting me, while my mom laughed at them. To shut them up, I probed about Dymond's mom again. "You heard my mom, how did your mom make out?"

"She's doing fine. Auntie Drama..." Porsha nudged Dymond. "I mean... Aunt Sapphire exaggerated a bit. My mom was banged up, but she's healing." Dymond summed it up.

"Oh, that's good. But umm, you still on punishment for lying to your mom right?" Manny and me started laughing and Dymond yelled out, "Porsha! No, you didn't tell him about that!"

Afterwards, we went outside to talk, me – Manny, Porsha, Kera and Dymond. The girls were acting funny like something was up; even Manny picked up on it.

"What happened when you went to see your P.O.?" Kera pried.

"I got 6 months probation."

"Shoot, that's good. You know Porsha only got forty hours of community service to complete."

"That's it?"

"Yeah, cleaning parks, streets, painting churches that sort of thing. That's all," Porsha shrugged, as it was nothing.

"So what y'all doing here? You rarely come by the store, what's up?" I asked her, looking over her shoulder towards Kera, Dymond and Manny who were watching us.

"Nothing. Do I need a reason to come see my baby-boo?" I could tell she was stalling.

"Unh-uh Porsha, you better tell him why we're here girl!" Kera shouted.

"Mind your business, Kera," Porsha mean mugged her.

"No, Porsha! You dragged us all the way down here; you better tell him or I will," Dymond added. "This is serious business."

"Dang! Excu-u-use me y'all," Porsha said sucking her teeth and rolling her eyes. Then she grabbed me by the arm and pulled me out of earshot of them.

"Ab, ..." Porsha said hesitantly.

"Spit it out, Porsha, what's going on?" By this time I was getting impatient.

"I think I'm pregnant," she said searching for my reaction. And boy! Was that a punch in the gut! I took a few seconds to catch my breath and regain my composure. I couldn't believe this was happening. If it weren't for bad luck, I wouldn't have any. I searched Porsha's eyes for a sign that she was joking, but I found none. Her pretty brown eyes were serious...very serious. "Well, let me correct that – I know I'm pregnant."

"What? How could?" My thoughts were scattered, as I stumbled for words to say.

"Sex at my house - condom broke – you remember? Don't get amnesia on me now!" I began to replay the conversation I had with Uncle Mark about being us being together when I went away to school. Was this her way of trying to hold onto me... to hold me back?

"Are you sure?" Porsha angrily cut me off saying,

"Don't start that, Abdul you're the only one I've been with, and you know it!"

79

"I don't know that for sure, I mean, there were rumors. But if you say it's mine, I guess I believe you."

She dug into her Coach bag that I bought for her and pulled out one of those home pregnancy tests. Yep, she was pregnant. *Unbelievable*, I thought to myself, yet here was the proof smacking me in the face. Oldheads say, "When it rains, it pours." Just when I resolve my court issues, I get another bomb dropped in my lap.

"So, what do you want to do, Porsha?" I knew what I wanted to do.

"What are you saying?"

So, I spoke flatly and got right to the point,
"I think you should have an abortion."

"You sure said that fast," she said, now upset with me. But I wasn't concerned about her feelings, I was thinking about our futures.

"Porsha, you're about to finish your first year of high school and I'm about to begin college. Neither of us are at a point in our lives to raise a baby. We are too young. Shoot, my mom still washes my clothes and cooks my dinner. If you have a better idea, please let me know."

She stood staring at me silently, with her hands on her hips in a sassy manner, as if she was about to curse me out. Then, the tears began to fall. I held her while she cried and dried her tears on my shirt.

"I'm sorry, Abdul; you're right. It's just the thought of having your baby felt kind of good. I was imagining us as a family... you know."

"Yea, I feel you, Porsha. But now isn't the time for that; we're not ready. Do you understand me?"

"Yes, now I have to figure out where I am going to get the money for an abortion."

"Hold up, have you talked to your mom about this? And, how much is this anyway?"

"Around $500. And, God no, she's already out to get you for getting me locked up!" My mind went to the $400 I had stashed away in my room for when I went away to college. My 'rainy day' money and if this wasn't a rainy day, I didn't know what was.

"Stay here, Porsha; I'll be right back." I rushed into my house running up the stairs to my bedroom. I got the last $400 out of my safety deposit shoebox and brought it downstairs. They were all grouped up talking amongst themselves. If my brother wasn't in the group, I would have thought there were conspiring against me. I pulled Porsha back off to the side.

"Here; that's $400. That should cover it."

She kissed my cheek and said, "Thank you, Abdul. I love you!"

Although I cared for her, I just wasn't in the mood to say it back.

"Do you want me to drive you to the abortion clinic?"

"No, it's really a nice day; we'll walk. I'll call you later," she said, walking off. I said bye to Kera and Dymond, as the three of them made their way up the street. I stood together with Manny watching them walking away, thinking that beauty definitely runs in their family. It was in 'dem jeans!

"Locked up and knocked up. What a combination!" I blew air from my mouth.

Chapter Thirteen

During the following days, everything went back to normal.
I dove back into my schoolwork. Howard High was busy as
seniors hustled to prepare for our upcoming graduation. A lot
of us were preparing to attend universities, community
colleges or technical institutions. Some were preparing to join
the Armed Forces or to enter the work force, while a small
amount weren't prepared for anything. They were just happy
to be out of school and ready to get their 'grown up' on.

With all of this positive behavior going on somehow a
few still found time to spread negative rumors. And it seemed
to me that Porsha's name was all in the rumor mill. I even
heard over at Newark they were talking about it. The 'so-
called' rumor about her and Jamal kept popping up. Although
I forced myself to ignore it, it was hard to overlook what
continued to surface. I got tired of complaining about it to
Porsha, who by the way was still my girl. I was determined to
not let the gossip come between us. I ran into Nat in between
classes. Since the incident with my car, our relationship had
been reduced to short greetings in passing. He was still my
man and I loved him like a brother, but he refused to stop
selling. He'd become the top dealer in our school since my
retirement.

"What's up, Nat?" I said, as our paths crossed.

"What's good, Abdul? I need to holla at you," Nat
said, walking with me down the hall.

"What's poppin'?" I asked, wondering if this had
anything to do with 'the business.'

"Same biz; what's up with you?"

"Nothing, just chillin'."

"How's your mom and pops?"

"Alright, and your pops?" Nat only lived with his father. His parents divorced when Nat was six years old.

"He's good. Umm..." he paused briefly. "Ab, do you still go out with Porsha?" Instantly, I anticipated bad news.

"Yeah, why?"

"I'm saying, cats around school have been talking. I'm not digging what I'm hearing, so you can't be feeling too good about it either," he explained.

"Man, that's just talk, you know how the haters are! Always on the negative stuff to bring you down."

"Nah, man, I'm not sure if it's just talk." Nat thinks like I do and he wouldn't repeat something to me, unless he was sure there was some truth to it. He wasn't like Manny who believed anything someone told him.

"What are you saying?" intensely, I asked.

"Man, I heard the same story from three different people and I thought it was strange that they all told the same lie. So, I began to think maybe it might not be a lie."

"Unless they all heard it from the same person," I said in defense of my girl.

"No, you don't understand. They're not telling what they heard, they're telling what they saw."

"What do you mean 'they saw'?"

"Check it out, they say that Jamal set Porsha up. He had two other guys hiding in his bedroom closet – watching them while he had sex with her!" That burned me up and honestly I believed it. I wanted to flip on somebody; I just didn't know who to flip on Jamal or Porsha?

"When did this supposedly happen?" I asked, wondering if I was in jail when this went down.

"I don't know. Do you want me to find out for you?" he offered.

"Yea, Nat. Good looking out, Dog," I said thankfully.

"Yo, Ab, I'm sure you're not trying to get into any trouble, so if you want me to beat Jamal down let me know and I got you." He really didn't like Jamal anyway.

"Naa, that's alright. That's love, kid – but I got this."

"Ai'ight, hold your head. I'll check you later and if you change your mind about Jamal, get at me."

"Ai'ight, Nat. One." I couldn't believe Porsha would be that stupid to play herself like that. I didn't want to accept it as the truth without checking it out first, but something in my mind told me that it was. I knew if I found out that she did have an encounter with Jamal that I'd have to let her go. If she did, I couldn't figure out what she thought she was doing. She had to know that she couldn't get away with it. If she was trying to get away with it, was the question that burned me up!

The whole situation had me twisted all day. The more I thought about it, the madder I got. It was more like a mixture of hurt and anger. I couldn't focus on anything in class. By the end of the day, when it was time to meet with coach, I was on edge. And I knew that Jamal would be in the gym. It was routine for us to keep sharp on our ball game when the season was over. I promised myself that I'd keep my cool and not snap while in the presence of the coach since he was one of the strongest influences to the scouts for me to obtain a scholarship. We went through the pick-up game without any incident. With Jamal sitting on the bench we didn't have any contact to flare up anything. But after the game – in the locker room, the drama was set and I could tell that it was about to unfold. I wasn't bothering this boy, I was getting dressed and here he came starting it up. Jamal and his boys were looking

84

through the new *Ridez* magazine. They were all talking loudly about which cars they wanted in the magazine, knowing they couldn't afford anything in there. Then Jamal said loudly, "How about a black Porsche? Any of you ever rode a black Porsche?" Everyone in the locker room got quiet, knowing that it was intended for me to see if I'd react. I didn't. I kept doing what I was doing as if I didn't ever hear him. I could see Manny out of the corner of my eye, gritting his teeth as he always does before he fights.

"Oh now, y'all don't *hear* me." Jamal said, pushing it, "What about you, Abdul? You ever ride in or on a black Porsche?" I didn't answer. "Well, I did," he bragged. "They're fast and easy to handle. They're just a little too expensive for my taste. You'd have to be stupid to spend that kind of money on a Porsche when you can always test it out... you know, for a joy ride. You feel me, Ab?" Jamal said, causing his boys to make ooh's and aah's sounds.

Manny jumped up, "Jamal, keep running your mouth and I'll give you what Ab gave you before. You see he ain't saying nothing back, but you insist on taking him there."

"Man, I don't care nothing about what you're saying and I don't care nothing about his feelings," Jamal pressed.

Manny rushed towards him and I caught his arm before he could reach Jamal. Everybody started shouting; people were holding Jamal back and I was holding Manny. It was chaos and I needed all my strength to hold Manny back. I grabbed our bags and had a few guys help me pull Manny out the gym.

On the ride home, Manny was hyped up in fight mode; he just couldn't let it go.

"I don't get you, Ab. Why do you keep letting that cat get away with talking slick?"

85

"He don't really want it. I already beat him down."

"Oh, it's clear that he does! He's been beating you down with words everyday."

"Words won't kill me."

"HE'S PLAYING YOU, MAN!" Manny yelled intensely. "I know he's getting to you!

I didn't answer, pretending to be concentrating on the road. The Anger Management class taught me to ignore it when someone is pushing your buttons. Almost every button had been pushed and I still maintain to keep calm, but I didn't know how long that would last. I had one last class to attend. I prayed that they would teach me an alternate method because I was at the end of my rope.

"I know you heard me. I bet you haven't even thought that it might be true. I told you she was all up in his face when you were locked up. You need to cut that girl off and stop letting both of them make a fool out of you!"

"You don't know for sure," I mumbled.

"How do you know? You weren't there, but rumor has it that two others were."

"Were you there?"

"Well, how come she hasn't been showing up to the gym? She used to always be there. If she was still down for you, she'd been there," he countered.

"She has community service after school; she can't come." I lied; her community service was over last week. Manny was silent for a while, getting frustrated. "I'm saying, Manny... I don't know if it's true... just like you don't. It ain't like I have proof," I told him.

"What more proof do you need? Man, the boy told you to your face! That's proof enough. What does this girl have on you? You got it bad! If you had proof," he said, putting me on the spot. "What would you do?"

"She'd have to go," I told him. He said no more after I said that. As we rode in silence, I searched my heart to see if I really meant what I told him. I believed that I did. It was a matter of how and where I was going to get the proof. I needed the kind of proof that I knew wasn't tainted by Jamal. If it was out there, I'd find it or it would find me. Until then, as far as I was concerned, Porsha was innocent until proven guilty.

I spotted Brittany in her travels. She waved to us and Manny told me to pull over.

"That's who you need to be with. Brittany has class. You never hear anybody talking bad about her."

"Be quiet! Since when you start knowing about the good girls?"

Brittany was dressed in a pair of jean capris with a T-shirt that said, Cutie Pie. That was an understatement. I don't know why I hadn't noticed her before.

"Guess what Ab?" she smiled brightly.

"What?" I answered nonchalantly.

"I got accepted to Syracuse!!"

"Word!" *Was this fate?* I wondered.

"That's good Brittany. You know that's where I'll be going."

"I know," she smiled even more. "Call me sometime – you have the number."

"A'ight, I'll get at you."

"Now, that's the brother I know! Playa, playa!" Manny was happier than I was.

Chapter Fourteen

After we arrived home, we both went about our chores in my parent's store without mention of the whole Porsha situation. But all that was running through my mind was, what if it's true? As much as I tried to think of other things, it always led back to her.

My dad and me were alone closing up the store that night and he noticed that I was drifting off.

"Hey, Chris... what planet are you on and how's life up there?" he clowned, referring to me being spaced out.

"Oh, I was just thinking, that's all, " I slowly replied.

"Sure, " he said.

"Hey, Dad? I know you're out of practice a bit, but I need some girl advice."

"Boy, ain't nothing out of practice about me. What's on your mind, son?"

"It's about Porsha. Well she... well I heard..." I stammered trying to figure out a clean way to explain a dirty rumor.

"Spit it out, son 'fore you choke on it," Dad said with a glint of humor in his eyes. I felt as if I was talking a futuristic, "old man" version of Manny.

"Well, I've been hearing rumors around school about Porsha; bad rumors. And I don't know what to do about it," I explained.

"Are the rumors true?"

"Don't know," I answered.

"What does she say about it?"

"She said it ain't true, but...."

"But what?"

"But everybody is saying it... including Manny and my boys."

"Well, tell me Chris, who does your trust lie with? Is it with the fellas?"

"No, but it's not with Porsha either." I replied without hesitation.

"Good, then here's my advice to you... follow your heart, but don't let it blind you," he told me and I wondered to myself what is that suppose to mean? Why do oldheads always give a solution to a problem in riddle form?

After we closed the store, we ate dinner. Once I finished, I went to my room to ponder my dad's advice. Sitting alone in my thoughts and Chris Brown's new CD, playing, *Yo – "Excuse me miss."* I fought off the urge to call her. But eventually she called me, as I expected she would. I didn't answer her call. I let the answering machine pick up and I listened to her message. She said something about her getting into a bad fight with Kera and she needed to talk to me 'cause she was stressing. *Well, too bad*, I thought to myself 'cause I was stressing too and it was all her fault. I dozed off early contemplating on what my dad said figuring out what he meant by "don't let it blind you."

At around three in the morning, I was awakened by Manny, who was sitting on my bed looking down at me. He was saying something that I couldn't make out 'cause everything was kind of foggy; I was half sleep.

"What?" I asked, sitting up in bed.

"I said Porsha has got to go," he demanded.

"Are you crazy, Manny? You didn't wake me up to tell me that. Boy, don't make me go upside your head," I said, rolling back over to go back to sleep.

89

"No, Ab, you don't understand. It's true. It's all true." He persisted by shaking me to keep me awake.

"What do you mean... how do you know it's true?" I asked. My heart was racing.

"I heard it from the most reliable source."

"Who?" Who could be more reliable than Porsha, herself, I wondered.

"Kera. She told me everything." My beating heart stopped – figuratively speaking. That was it. I knew that whatever info Kera had, must've come from the horse's mouth.

"What did she say?" I asked, as my throat began to dry up and constrict from nervousness.

"What didn't she say? Well, let me start from the top..." Manny began, grasping my full attention, " Kera and Porsha got into some kind of fight; I don't know what it was about..."

"Yea, Porsha left me a message earlier to tell me about it," I cut in.

"Right. So, Kera calls me mad and loose-lipped. It took a little expert coaxing on my behalf, but I got her to spill the beans," Manny said proudly.

"Stop feeling yourself and tell me what she said."

"Well, the day when she came here with Kera and Dymond to tell you that she was pregnant – and you gave her $400 for an abortion – was the day Kera found out. Which by the way, you forgot to mention to me," Manny frowned.

"It was none of your business. Besides, I thought Kera told you."

"Well, she didn't. Anyway, it turns out, that on the way home Porsha explained everything to them. When Porsha found out that she was pregnant, she knew automatically that the baby wasn't yours," Manny explained.

"No, you're wrong about that. We had sex and the condom broke."

"Maybe so, but Kera said she had her period after you two engaged. Then she had unprotected sex with Jamal while you were locked up, which was when he had all those boys hiding in the closet."

"So, it's true." I was speaking more to myself than I was to Manny.

"You darn right it's true. But hold up, it gets worse," Manny continued.

"What can be worse?" I said under my breath.

"Check it out, when she found out she was pregnant, she stepped to Jamal about it. He said it's not his business and he wasn't giving her any money for an abortion. He told her to go to you and tell you it was yours, so you could pay for it 'cause dude said we got money. Check how dirty Porsha is… after she got the money from you, she told Kera and Dymond about it."

My high school sweetheart pulled the wool over my eyes! I was hot! I felt like a natural born sucker. I couldn't believe she would play me like that. I mean, she played me all around the board. First, she had an encounter with my enemy. I knew I shouldn't have had sex with her in the first place! Why didn't I listen when my mom was preaching abstinence? If I did, I wouldn't be involved in this mess! Having sex with her was not worth all of this confusion in my life. Not only that, Porsha had me running around naïve, while she continued to lie to me. Darn near everybody in school is laughing at me behind my back. To top it off – she conspired with my enemy on how to beat me for $400! She followed through with it too.

91

She lied in my face, performing like an Oscar winning actress. Now my dad's advice made all the sense in the world. I was definitely letting my eyes blind me. No, no... it was this *Grimey* chick, Porsha who had me *Blinded*. Not anymore! From this time forward, my eyes were wide open. Manny had said something, but I didn't hear him.

"What?"

"I asked you what are you gonna do?"

They played me so many ways, all that was left was the million dollar question – what was I gonna do? My first instinct was to beat both of them, deliver the same pain that I was feeling – whether it was physically or mentally. Only problem was that Porsha was a female. My father always taught us that any man who hits a woman is not a man. He told us there was no excuse for a man to hit a woman, whatsoever. So as much as I wanted to punch her in the mouth, me hitting her was not an option.

"I'm cutting Porsha off; she's done!"

"And Jamal? You already let him get away with too much." The little voice inside my head had already told me what to do.

"Don't worry about Jamal; I'll handle him."

Manny got up and went back to bed, but not without a warning. "You make sure you do 'cause I'm not letting it slide. He violated and he's gonna get it; even if I have to give it to him."

After Manny left, I laid in my bed sleepless for the remainder of the morning. Eventually, I got up showered and dressed, ready for school. By the time Manny got up, I was already on my way out the door. He'd have to catch the bus to school this morning, I thought, 'cause I had some serious business to handle. I jumped in my car and headed towards

92

Porsha's crib. Although I was awake the majority of the night, I wasn't tired. I was charged up and very much anticipating the jump-off. Pulling in front of her house, I beeped the horn several times before she came running out with her bag and jumped in the passenger's seat. Leaning over to kiss me on my cheek, I was cold as ice, non-responsive.

"What's up, baby? I called you last night; I got the machine."

"Word."

"Yeah, your girl was going through something. I needed a shoulder to cry on."

"Why didn't you just call Jamal?"

"That's not funny, Ab," she replied.

"It wasn't meant to be."

"Come on, Ab. I know you're not letting that gossip get to you again."

"Don't play with me, Porsha! You've disrespected me enough! It's time to come clean." Now, I was heated. Here she was continuing this game of charades, fronting on me like I was a fool.

"What are you?..."

I cut her off, "Porsha, I already know. I know everything... even about Jamal being the father. The cat is out of the bag. It's time to keep it gutter, Porsha. Be a young lady and show *some* self-respect."

"Abdul, I love *youuu!*" She started crying fake tears, but that wasn't gonna fly this time; I was beyond that.

"That's all you have to say to me? Well, I don't love you, Porsha... I don't even like you. Right now you disgust me! All I'm asking is for you to tell the truth and you can't do that. You owe me the truth!" This was pouring from my heart.

"I could've had any girl I wanted, but I choose you and you played me!"

Then she spoke up, "Abdul, I'm so sorry. I never meant for us to turn out like this. Please believe me, I never intended to hurt you."

Even though I didn't believe her, I just had to know, "Why? Why'd you do it?"

"When you were locked up, I was just chilling and hanging with Jamal and his boys one day. I was chillin' with them, trying to maul things out in my mind. Jamal was there in my head telling me about all the different cheerleaders you've been messing with. I was hurt and he was there to comfort me. After that, when you came home, I was trying to cover things up. But it just kept getting worse. My lie kept getting bigger.

"What about the pregnancy thing? Why did you blatantly lie to me, huh? Explain that!" I was so disgusted; I didn't even want to look at her.

"Well..." she continued her little story, "when Jamal mentioned it to me, it made sense to me; at the moment, anyway. I knew you were a good guy, responsible... and I needed the money right away. I couldn't tell my mom; she doesn't believe in abortions. And, you were right; I'm too young to have a baby. I just couldn't do that. After you gave me the money, I felt bad. I told Kera and Dymond when we left your parent's store the real deal, 'cause I knew it would get back to you through Kyle or Manny; being that I couldn't bring myself to tell you. That was my way of letting you know."

"How noble of you," I said sarcastically.

"Ab, I'm so sorry about it all. I'll pay you back the $400 if that will help anything," she said. The girl who I cared for was a deceiving tramp and thinking about no one but

94

herself. With all that I recently went through, I felt as though she never really had my best interest at heart. I knew what time it was time to kick her to the wind. With the quickness, I pulled over to the curb and threw the car in park. I turned in my seat, facing her. "Listen to me, girl; listen closely and don't interrupt me. I loved you more than any cat you've ever been with. You were a nobody...a freshman chick when I met you; but I didn't see none of that or hold it against you. I saw 'Porsha' and I accepted you as you were. I did everything for you and in return you not only violated me, you also helped Jamal, violate me."

"But... but, Ab..."

"Don't! Let me finish! I just want you to know that I'm not mad at you anymore. In fact, I'm kind of thankful that you freed me. Now, I can go away to school without having you on my mind. I only hope that you've learned from this experience, 'cause I learned something. I learned that no good deed goes unpunished. Now get out of my car. See ya!" With that, I used the switch on my door panel to unlock hers.

"You mean get out right here?" The school was a mile away.

"Yep, now, GET 'TA STEPPIN', before I violate my father's rules and square you in your mouth," I demanded. Still in Hollywood form, she got out, closed the door and leaned over to look in the window banging on the hood of the car.

"Ab, please don't do this..." was all I heard. I pulled off, leaving her standing on the curb, in disbelief looking at the exhaust from my car.

Chapter Fifteen

After kicking Porsha to the curb, I drove to school and parked. I parked purposely near the entrance I knew that Jamal and his boys used. It was still kind of early; most of the students were just showing up for first period. I turned on the radio and waited – patiently. I was on a destructive journey from an emotional rollercoaster; even the Anger Management techniques didn't work. I didn't have a real plan on what I was going to say or do to Jamal, 'cause I wasn't as angry as when I first found out – I was bitter! I waited. *He kept disrespecting me!* I watched... I watched and I waited. *He used my girl as a weapon to ridicule me!* I played it over and over in my head. Then, I spotted him in my rearview mirror. The punk was headed for another entrance, walking with a cheerleader. His boys were close, also walking behind him with other cheerleaders. I didn't expect him to use that entrance; I almost missed him. I hurried out of the car and rushed over to where Jamal was, in hopes of catching him before he entered the school.

"Now what do we have here?" Jamal sneered to his boys when he noticed me jogging their direction.

"Let me have a word with you, Jamal," I said calmly, but furiously.

"Can somebody tell me why is this cat always showing up where I'm at? Do you have a crush on me, Abdul?" he jeered at me, stimulating everyone within earshot to laugh.

"I didn't come here to play games with you Jamal; I came to get my money."

"What money are you talking about?" he asked with a real stupid, screwed smirk on his face that told me he knew exactly what I was talking about.

Stepping closer to him, I firmly said, "I'm talking about the money I gave Porsha to abort your little rug-rat she was carrying around."

"Ohhh... you mean your wife and *my* kid. Why didn't you just say that?" he joked, entertaining everyone to laugh again.

"Four... you owe me four hundred, Jamal," I said with a tight face, not smiling at his lame jokes.

"Whoa! Abdul... you gave her four Benjamins? It's that *easy*? Well look, I'm pregnant too and it's your baby – I need four hundred." Jamal joked holding his stomach and back, imitating a pregnant woman.

"Last chance, Jamal. Are you going to give me my money or not?" I demanded, fed up with his clowning.

"Not! Now what? What!" Speaking loudly, he stepped closer with his grill inches from mine.

"Now for Plan B." *WHOPP!!!!* I suckered punched him. After that, I whacked him again. He swung back and we went at it like cats and dogs. With him being the cat: I was definitely the dog... a vicious PIT BULL! For all the rumors and gossip I had to endure, for all his jokes, ridicule and verbal abuse, for creeping with my girl, for getting her pregnant and having her blame me... for everything in a nutshell I gave it to him! I beat him down worse than I did the

97

first time and this time nobody broke it up. Kicking, punching, kneeing, elbowing, body-slamming and slapping him up and down the block like a girl for ten minutes straight, until just the very thought of me knocking him around got tired. I could have gone a few more minutes beating on the punk, but why? I stood over him cowering on the ground, thinking if I wanted to whip that fool again. It wasn't the solution to our conflict, but it temporarily fixed my need to address him properly.

"Okay...okay... you got it, Ab... that's it... please," through swollen lips he pleaded, "I don't want to fight anymore... just don't..."

"I know I got it!" I interrupted him. "...and for the record, you bum, can keep the $400 and Porsha too, enjoy yourself." Turning to walk away, the gathered crowd parted for me like the Red Sea, clearing a path for me to get through. Passing through the crowd, I caught several students who nodded their heads in agreement, as a sign of respect. Most knew Jamal had it coming to him and I just gave them something else to talk about.

"Ab! Watch your back!" I recognized that voice. It was Brittany from afar. Turning around, Jamal seven feet away from me, and approaching fast. In his hand was a gun. A gun – he had a gun! Searching for a place to run, there was none. Now, I was desperate for a place to hide. He was too close; and even with my speed, I couldn't out run bullets. I knew in my heart and saw it in his eyes; he was going to shoot me. And why not, I just openly beat him down in front of a crowd. My mom always says, "Violence begets violence." It's a never-ending cycle and here it is back to return the favor to me. I didn't know my heart could beat so fast. I wondered to myself, *when he kills me, will I feel it?*

Jamal enraged, shouted, "GET ON YOUR KNEES, ABDUL!!!"

"Look Jamal, we can…"

"I SAID GET ON YOUR KNEES OR I SWEAR I'LL KILL YOU THIS VERY SECOND!" He immediately cocked back the hammer on the gun. *Where did he get a gun? Did he keep one in school? Was it in his car? Or, did one of his boys give it to him?*

The crowd began clearing out of the way; no one wanted to get hit by a stray bullet that was meant for me. I guess I couldn't blame them, I thought as I got on one knee. Jamal stepped in closer and pressed the barrel of the gun to my forehead. The steel was as cold as my heart was when I was beating him down, but now he possessed the same rage. Before I was the one blind with rage. Could my dad foresee this? Porsha blinded me in more ways than one. I was a young fool caught up in puppy love that had me jeopardizing my future and once again, for what?… a girl?

"Jamal, you don't wanna…." I began my plea.

"SHUT UP! I didn't say you could speak. You're gonna learn that whenever you come against me, you can't win. Class in session." With that said, he kick me in face. I fell hard from the blow and he took full advantage of me being down. Then by the grace of God, he forced me on my feet, with the threat of his gun pointing at me. Where were the teachers when I needed them?

"IF I CATCH YOU AGAIN, AB… IT'LL BE WORST THAN THE LAST TIME!" he shouted behind me, as I ran towards my car. Bruised and running, I knew in my heart what I was prepared to do. I wasn't thinking rational; too late for that. All rational thoughts were evaporated and no hopes of returning. *He wants to play with guns? I'll show him how to play with guns,* I thought, recklessly. I ran into Manny and Kyle on the way to my car. They'd arrived at school the same time. One look at my battered face and torn clothes spoke volumes, leaving them staring at me with their mouths open.

"What happened to you?" Manny asked.

"Jamal happened," I replied, walking angrily past him towards my car.

"Well, why are you going that way? Come on, we're gonna jump him," Manny flatly stated, starting to walk toward the direction I just came from.

"Manny!" I called after him. Manny and Kyle both turned to see what I wanted.

"What?"

"He's got a gun," I warned them. "Jamal... Jamal has a gun," I cautioned again.

"Then, what are you waiting for? Let's get out of here!" Manny ordered walking towards me, and then passed me. He wasn't punkin' out but he wasn't no fool either. When a dude has a gun you better walk, no better yet, run away and fast!

"Kyle, you might as well go ahead to school. You don't have any beef with Jamal. I'll call you later to see what's going on in school, alright?" I knew he didn't want to really get mixed up with this.

"Alright,' he agreed, seeming to be relieved. Kyle's father was the principal. It would've been all over the headlines... 'The first African-American Principal of Howard High son was arrested at school with an illegal weapon with the intent to harm another student! What an example he is!'

In my mind, I knew how to end this permanently. On the ride to our house, I explained to Manny what happened between me and Jamal, and what I intended to do about it. Blood was coming down my face. Manny unbuttoned his shirt and removed his wife-beater to tie around my head. I looked up in the rear view mirror – my face was busted!

When we arrived home, my parents were in the store, so it was easy for us to enter the side door without them noticing us. My car was also parked out of view. Once inside, I headed straight for my parent's room to grab the gun I knew my dad kept stashed in a box in the top of his closet. A few years back, our store was robbed at gunpoint. So, my brother Tyrone gave my dad a gun to keep in the store. But ever since my brother was killed, Dad never brought the gun down to the store anymore. It stayed collecting dust in that box in his closet. I checked the gun to see if it was loaded, then I stuffed it down my waistline. Next, I walked into my room, sat on my bed and prayed that I didn't get caught.

"What are you going to do with that?" Manny asked, pointing to Dad's gun.

"What do you THINK I'm doing with it?"

"Put that gun back, Ab. We don't need that."

"What do you mean we don't need it? He has a gun," I retorted, thinking out of anger.

"So?"

"So, I'm fighting fire with fire."

"No, you're fighting stupidity with stupidity."

"Look, Manny; he started this. He brought guns into the picture, I didn't. Now I'm gonna show him ain't nothing sweet about Abdul."

"How? How are you gonna show him that? By getting killed, or killing him, and spending the rest of your life in jail? It's a 'no-win' situation anyway you look at it."

"I won't get caught," I said stupidly.

"You think you can shoot him in front of a bunch of people and get away with it?"

"It's a strong possibility!" At the moment, none of that mattered to me; I was so angry, I didn't care. Manny could preach all he wanted, but it didn't happen to him. He didn't have a gun pulled out on him. He didn't have a gun pressed to his face – I did. I got kicked in the face and ridiculed like a punk in front of people... even, Brittany. I had to tuck my tail between my legs and run like a coward. He didn't understand. He didn't know what I was feeling. "I feel you, Manny. I hear what you're saying; but you're not hearing me. What you're saying is probably right - all of it. But that's not where my mind is right now. Right now, I just don't care."

"So, you gon' throw it all away because of some girl. What is it that you don't care about, huh?"

"I don't care about right or wrong; I don't care about life or death; I don't care about consequences... I don't care about making it right now," I sourly stated.

"How about me?"

"What about you?"

"Do you care about me? Do you care about mom and dad? Do you care about Uncle Mark? Most importantly, do you care that our brother died by a man full of rage with a gun? What about yourself? Do you care about yourself?" I didn't answer and I didn't think he asked to get a response. Whatever his intentions were, his questions had me second-guessing my actions. But the images of the morning's events continued to replay in my mind, adding fuel to the fire raging inside me.

"Manny, fall back... you don't understand where I'm at right now. Just be easy; I got this."

"You're right, Ab. I don't understand. Let's call Uncle Mark and ask him how should we handle this."

"Oh, now you want to call the cops on me?" I asked, alarmed.

"Since when did Uncle Mark become 'the cops'?"

"Since, he became my probation officer, the only link to me going back to jail!"

"As I recall, he was the only link to get your butt out of jail."

"Yea. Yea. Whatever. Do what you got to do and I'm gonna do what I gotta do; that's all it is."

"And what are you gonna do, Ab?"

"I'm going back to school and bang Jamal," I said without question.

"You're stupid. All that talk you talk about me is nothing, but talk! Practice what you preach! See what that girl got you involved in! She's not worth it man. What about what Fabian told you? I guess you forgot about jail that quick," Manny shouted and stormed out of my room.

I sat back and watched the clock tick, waiting on the hour of recognition. Jamal opened a can of worms when he pulled that gun on me. I was about to teach him that he should always finish what he starts.

Chapter Sixteen

I was in route – back to school. This time, I parked in a different spot. I checked and re-checked my dad's gun. I didn't want anything to go wrong when I ran up on Jamal. Checking the time, I took out my cell and called Kyle to see what was going on inside the school building.

"Hello," Kyle answered his cell.

"Kyle, it's me."

"Oh… what up, Ab? You know everybody's talking. Jamal got nabbed with the gun. As soon as I went inside the school, I informed my dad. The police came and arrested him. Don't come back up here man or, you'll get arrested too."

"They won't catch me," I said stubbornly.

"Let it go man. This is not you. Don't throw your life away. You have a full ride to Syracuse, why would you mess that up? The judge gave you another chance. Don't be like that guy named Fabian that you told me about. He'll never see daylight again." I just hung up the phone on him. This was the second time Fabian's name was mentioned. Kyle was also right; this wasn't me. Flashbacks of my conversation with Fabian came to me. I'd let Jamal take me out of my zone just like the teacher in Anger Management warned me of – "Never let them take you out your zone. You may end up doing something you'll regret later in life." I stooped to his level of ignorance and was prepared to throw my life away again for nothing! I uncocked the hammer on the gun, put the safety latch on and drove back home. I cried all the way there.

Uncle Mark, my mom and dad were getting inside of the car when I pulled up. Dad rushed over to the car and pulled me out forcefully.

"WHERE IS THE GUN?"

I handed it to him and fell into his arms and cried. I think this was the first time I cried that hard since my brother Tyrone was murdered.

"I'm proud of you son and so would Tyrone be. It took a big man to back down."

Manny came over and joined in the embrace.

"Thank you lil' bro for talking sense into me."

"Man, charge it to the game," he grinned. "Oh for real though, you need to get on your job and start being a better role model for me." Uncle Mark came over and popped him upside the head. My mom had her head in her bosom crying.

There is a limit to which a person could be pushed before they'd snap out. Which doesn't mean that, that person has gone crazy, it only means one has taken leave of their normal faculties, such as common sense and listening to reason. My listening to reason came from another – Fabian. This was someone who had been down the same road, but with a different outcome.

Epilogue

With time, everything worked out okay. I finished my last days of school in peace. Jamal was expelled and unable to graduate. Of course, there were many rumors going around, but don't they always? They never stop. It seemed that by not shooting Jamal, I demonstrated bravery. I accepted that shooting him would've been the cowardly way out, making a bad situation even worse.

My boy Nat continued to sell and he eventually escalated on to selling other drugs. He quickly became one of the biggest drug dealers in our neighborhood. We chatted, but only when he was clean, which was rare. I was however, concerned about his well-being 'cause I knew the ending for the song he choose to sing. When he continuously failed to listen to me, I had to stand back and let him sing his song.

That summer before I went off to the Syracuse, I asked one favor of Uncle Mark. I asked him to find someone for me. I asked him to find my 'voice of reason.' Fabian, who's full name was Fabian Gibson, was serving a 40-year sentence for murder. He was still in the juvenile facility, but when he turned eighteen he'd be shipped to an adult prison. Uncle Mark took us to visit him. I explained to him all that I'd been through since I had gotten out. I thanked him for the lessons he gave me. We only returned to see him once more after the first visit to bring him some food, money and clothes. A small gesture in comparison to what he gave me – knowledge, which I'd use for the rest of my life.

Brittany and I talked more often and were both ready for college. When Porsha found out that we were talking, she blew up my phone! Guess what? I never would answer. You can imagine the messages she left. But hey, she had me first, but she messed up. I heard that she was still seeing Jamal after all of that. I'm not sure how true it is – could be another rumor – who knows? I'm not sticking around to find out. I guess neither one of them learned a lesson. But that's *another* story.

Manny and Kera were still dating, but Manny watched her closely after what Porsha did. He didn't have too much worry though because they still weren't speaking.

Kyle was still trying to get Dymond to be his girl, but Miss Dymond In The Rough was still playing hard. She told him she didn't want to rush into anything; they could remain friends.

Just before I was set to leave I got bad news, my boy Nat got caught up in a DEA – Drug Enforcement Agency sting. They raided his dad's home and found a bunch of drugs in his garage that Nat stashed there. Nat manned-up and took the responsibility for the drugs so his father wouldn't have to go to jail. But that's *another* story.

And me… well, in four years, I'll be headed for the NBA; first round, second draft-pick, starting point guard… Christopher 'Abdul' Parker. With a new chick on my side… maybe! But that's *another* story.

Holla at cha' boy!

Please visit and join the youth group at:
http://groups.yahoo.com/group/precioustymesyg/

Book One
Dymond In The Rough

Book Two
The AB-solute Truth

Platinum Teen Series

Coming soon…

Book Three
Best Kept Secret

Book Four
Runaway

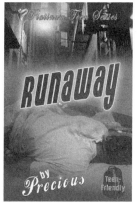

Platinum Teen Series

Also check out...

Teenage Bluez

Teen Issues that get Real Crazy....

Accustomed to the sheltered life, Ricky Coleman yearns to be accepted into the crowd. Soon he goes from study hall to hanging with a feared neighborhood criminal. Influenced by his thugged out boy Marco, Ricky finds himself in a police chase that could seal his fate. Will this pretty boy survive the hard life of a Juvenile detainee?

Helplessly in love with an older man, Niyah Christian, 17 falls into a double trap. Malik, a suave newcomer wines and dines her into a web of deception. Once ripped from the safety of her family and best friend Denim, she finds herself lost and turned out. With no where to turn, Niyah hits rock bottom.

Bria, the daughter of a famous pro football player learned early that money is power and a sure sign of success. While she embraces the life of the wealthy and elite, her girl Tiff from the hood, is hot to trot and on her way to a life filled with pain. Will their friendship last?

Visit www.lifechangingbooks.net to find out more about **Teenage Bluez**.
ISBN: 0-9741394-9-1

JOIN THE PLATINUM TEEN FAN CLUB!!

Precioustymes Entertainment
C/O Platinum Teens
229 Governors Place, #138
Bear, DE 19701
Email us at: precioustymesent@aol.com

Are you a teen writer with a strong desire to get published?

If so, contact us!
Join the Platinum Teen movement!